Planning perfect weddings...
finding happy endings!

It's the biggest and most important day of
a woman's life—and it has to be perfect.

At least that's what The Wedding Belles
believe, and that's why they're Boston's
top wedding planner agency. But amidst
the beautiful bouquets, divine dresses
and rose petal confetti, these six wedding
planners long to be planning
their own big day!

But first they have to find Mr Right...

This month: Shirley Jump
SWEETHEART LOST AND FOUND
Florist: will Callie catch a bouquet, and
reunite with her childhood sweetheart?

And don't miss the exciting wedding
planner tips and author reminiscences
that accompany each book!

Shirley tells all about her own big day:

"You seriously can't take me anywhere without a calamity happening. I'm a walking *America's Funniest Home Videos*. Even my own wedding had a near-disaster. My husband got laryngitis the day of the wedding (hmmm, was that a convenient way of not having to say any vows?), so his vows came out as a squeak. I forgot our toasting glasses, and we had to borrow other guests' champagne glasses when the best man made his speech.

But all of that was nothing compared to my veil catching on fire.

Let's just say tulle and candles aren't a good mix. When my husband and I went to blow out the unity candle, it was before he kissed me, so my veil was still down. I tried to blow through the tulle. The netting swooped forward into the flame and, *whoosh*, caught on fire. Not a big flame, thank goodness, but a nice little spark. So there I was, madly blowing out my veil, then trying to lift the veil and get the unity candle blown out at the same time. I have a nice round hole in my veil as a memento.

Don't even get me started on the time I tripped and fell on the church altar in front of two hundred people at someone else's wedding. And just don't ask me to do a reading at your wedding—not unless you're planning on splitting the prize money from *AFHV* with me.

At least in my fictional world of SWEETHEART LOST AND FOUND I can create weddings where almost nothing goes wrong!"

Catch up with Shirley's latest news at www.shirleyjump.com

SWEETHEART
LOST AND FOUND

BY
SHIRLEY JUMP

MILLS & BOON
Pure reading pleasure

*To Kathy, who has brought music and laughter into our lives,
and who graciously forgave me for tripping on the altar
in the middle of her wedding.*

First published in Great Britain 2008
Harlequin Mills & Boon Limited,
Eton House, 18-24 Paradise Road, Richmond, Surrey TW9 1SR

© Shirley Kawa-Jump, LLC 2008

ISBN: 978 0 263 86510 3

Set in Times Roman 12¾ on 14¼ pt
02-0408-51103

Printed and bound in Spain
by Litografia Rosés, S.A., Barcelona

Callie Stevens is the florist at The Wedding Belles. Here are her tips for your big day:

❦ A little visual can go a long way toward making sure you and the florist are on the same page. So bring along pictures of floral arrangements you like, or flowers you find special, to give your florist an image of the perfect bouquet.

❦ If you get married around a holiday, remember that the church will probably already be fully decked out with great flowers. Save some money by utilizing the beautiful setting already in place.

❦ To save money, don't go for cheap flowers—choose one striking bloom in a less expensive vase arrangement for a centerpiece, or a simple bouquet with a few colorful flowers. Sometimes less is more.

❦ On the big day, be sure someone has been designated to be in charge of distributing and pinning on the boutonnieres and corsages so you don't have to worry about that detail.

❦ If you want your guests to be able to see each other across the table, be sure to keep centerpieces under 14 inches high. Also, keep highly fragrant flowers to a minimum at table settings, for guests who might have scent allergies.

CHAPTER ONE

CALLIE Phillips slipped the final flower into the cheery wedding bouquet, stepped back to admire her handiwork and marveled at the irony of her career choice.

A woman who didn't believe in happily ever after, crafting floral dreams for starry-eyed, Cinderella-was-no-fairy-tale brides.

Callie fingered the greenery surrounding the flowers symbolizing hope. True love. A happy ending. Her clients at Wedding Belles were paying her to act like she believed fairy tales came true. But all the while Callie created those dreams with vibrant blooming white roses and delicate pastel freesia, she hid the fact that the petals had long ago dropped from her own jaded heart.

"My goodness, will you look at that. Another beautiful creation, darlin'." Belle Mackenzie, the owner of the Wedding Belles and Callie's employer, breezed into the basement floral design area. She was impeccable as always in a skirt and bright red sweater set that offset her gray hair and shaved years off her fifty-plus age. "You are incredible. Whatever made you think of this combination?" Belle bent to inhale the fragrance of the burnt-orange tulips, paired with deep purple calla and crimson gloriosa lilies.

"The bride, actually," Callie said. "Becky was just so outgoing, and this design seemed to suit her personality, not to mention the unique colors of her wedding party dresses."

"I don't know how you do it. You read people like novels." Belle smiled. "Best thing I ever did was hire you."

Callie smiled. "No, I think it's the opposite. Best thing I ever did was walk in here and apply for a job." Belle had taken Callie under her wing years ago, seeing a budding creative talent and someone who needed a stable, maternal figure. She'd taught Callie the art of flower arranging, even paid for her to go to classes, then when she'd expanded her wedding planning company into the much bigger Wedding Belles, had given Callie the job of florist. And through that job, a group of close friends who had since become Callie's rock.

Giving Callie's unstable life a firm basis for the first time in her life.

Now Callie spent her days discussing calla lilies and Candia roses with starry-eyed brides, but never for one moment believing she would hold another bouquet, opening her heart a second time, believing once again that one man would be by her side forever.

Just the idea of forever made her consider heading for the hills. She'd tried it once, on a whim, and it hadn't worked at all. Callie wasn't slipping on that gold band of permanence again under any circumstances.

Belle gave her a grin. "We all make a good team, don't we? The Wedding Belles."

"Even if one of us has never been swayed to the dark side?"

Belle's laughter was hearty. "You mean the white side of the aisle? It's not as bad as you think over there. And one day, darlin', I'll convince you that falling in love and getting married isn't the prison sentence you think."

Ever since Belle had hired her three years ago, she'd been working on convincing Callie that marriage was an institution for everyone, sort of like a One Size Fits All suit. Callie wasn't surprised—the gregarious owner of the wedding planner company had been married several times and had gone into the business because she loved happy endings. The other women on the Belles team echoed that sentiment—and most had already found their happily ever after.

But Callie knew better. For some people, love was an emotion best left for greeting cards.

"Belle, I already tried marriage once and it didn't work." Callie cut the end of the crimson satin ribbon that she'd tied in a ballet slipper style around the stems of the bouquet, then tucked a few strands of reflective wires and delicate crystal sprays into the flowers, adding a touch of bling.

"That's called practice," Belle said, laughing. "Second time's always better. And if not, third time's a charm. Or in my case, maybe the fourth."

Callie rolled her eyes. "I'm certainly not going to get married that many times." If at all, ever again. Her divorce was only eighteen months in the past, and if there was one thing her marriage to Tony had taught Callie—

It was that she, of all people, should never get married again.

"You know what you should do?" Belle said. "Celebrate."

"Celebrate what?"

"Being single again. You've been back on the market for over a year, Callie, and you have yet to take a step out of the barn."

"A step out of the barn?"

"And pick another stallion in the corral." Belle

winked. "There are plenty of 'em out there, honey. All you need to do is pick the one that gets your hooves beatin' the fastest."

"Oh, no, not me." Callie waved off the idea, even as she laughed at Belle's advice. "I'll keep on working with the flowers. They don't let me down."

"They also don't keep your bed toasty at night."

"So I'll buy an electric blanket." Callie put the bouquet, along with the rest of the wedding party flowers, inside the large walk-in refrigerator, then turned to walk upstairs with Belle. In a couple of hours, she and the other Belles would deliver everything to the wedding party, and see one more bride down the aisle.

"Well, before you go choosing a blanket over a beau, will you run on down to O'Malley's tonight and drop off the new invitations for his daughter's wedding? Apparently the first time the printer changed the groom's name from Clarence to Clarice. Thankfully we caught the mistake just before they got mailed."

Callie eyed Belle. "Is this some way of forcing me out?"

Belle gave a suspicious up and down of her shoulders, a teasing smile playing at her lips. "Maybe."

Audra Green, the company's accountant,

greeted the two of them as they entered the reception area of the Belles' office. The entire room spoke of Belle's sunny personality, with its bright yellow walls, gleaming oak floors and bright white woodwork. It welcomed and warmed everyone who entered, just as Belle herself did. "What's Belle cooking up now?" Audra asked. "I read something mischievous in her eyes."

"Proving to Callie that Mr. Right could be right down the street."

"Along with the Easter Bunny and Santa Claus," Callie deadpanned, retrieving the box of invitations from the desk.

"So I thought she should go down to O'Malley's tonight and maybe deliver these invitations, scope out the dating scene," Belle went on, optimistically ignoring Callie. "Get back on the horse before she forgets where the stirrups are."

Callie and Audra laughed, then the straitlaced accountant sobered and gave Callie a sympathetic smile. "Do you want some company?" Audra asked.

"Thanks, but I won't need it. Contrary to Belle's matchmaking plans, I'm going to drop off these wedding invitations and nothing more," Callie said.

"And if Mr. Right happens to be sitting at the end of the bar?" Belle asked.

"If he is," Callie laughed at Belle's indomitable belief in Disney endings and picked up one of the thick silver envelopes in the box and wagged it in Belle's direction for emphasis, "then I'm sure you'll be the first to announce it to the world."

Jared Townsend believed in the power of proof. If something could be proved beyond a shadow of a doubt, then he accepted it as fact.

His quest for proof was why he had excelled in geometry but not abstract thought. Why he'd nearly failed poetic analysis and instead discovered a home in the concrete world of statistics.

But now he found himself in the most unlikely of places, to prove the most unprovable of statistics. A bar on a Thursday night.

To prove that true love could be measured and analyzed, weighed and researched. For that reason, he had a clipboard and a pen and intended to interview at least a dozen couples before the bar closed, assuming he stayed awake that long.

A party animal, he was not. He wasn't even a party puppy.

"Welcome to O'Malley's. What can I get you?" A rotund bartender with a gray goatee came over to Jared, a ready smile on his face, his hand already on a pint glass. At the other end of the bar sat an older man, his shoulders hunched, head hung, staring into a beer.

"Beer sounds good." Jared slid his clipboard onto the bar, along with a few already sharpened pencils. Raring to go.

If anything spelled geek, that was it. No wonder Jared hadn't had a date in three months. Carry a clipboard—an instant death knell for attracting women.

The bartender arched a brow at the pencils and clipboard, apparently agreeing with that mental assessment, but kept his counsel and poured the draft. He slid the frosty mug over to Jared without a word.

A couple walked in. Jared grabbed a pencil, readying himself. At first glance, they looked perfect for his survey. Early twenties, blond girl, brunette guy, walking close, talking fast, as if they were—

Arguing.

"You're a moron," the girl said. "I don't know what I ever saw in you. Seriously, Joey, my toaster has more brains than you and that's *after* I burned my bagel."

"Dude, that's mean."

"And quit calling me dude. I'm your *girl*friend, or at least I was. Not your dude." She flung off his hand and stalked away, ordering a tequila shot, which she knocked back in one swift, easy movement that said she'd done this before. More than once.

Jared put down his pencil. He let out a sigh, settled back on his stool and took a long, deep gulp of beer. No one else was in the bar, even though it was nearly nine and the sign outside promised karaoke night would start in a little while. Maybe he should have picked a place further downtown, rather than one so close to his apartment.

"Hey, O'Malley, how 'bout another for the road?" the man sitting at the opposite end of the bar said. He raised his glass, but it trembled and he nearly dropped it.

"I think you've had enough," the bartender, apparently the O'Malley namesake of the bar, said.

The man swayed in his seat. "No, no. Not enough, not yet."

Jared heard the words—so familiar—and turned away, fiddling with his clipboard. His memory raced back all the same to someone else, to another slurred voice, determined to have one more round.

O'Malley let out a grunt of disgust. "You're cut off. Why don't you go home?"

"Don't wanna go home." The man heaved a sigh, stumbled off the stool and careened down the bar. "No one there. No one t'all." He crashed into a couple more stools, then gripped the edge of the polished oak surface and teetered.

The memories slammed into Jared until he couldn't ignore them any longer. He shook his head, then got to his feet and caught the man's elbow, righting the stranger just before he lost his balance.

"Get him some coffee," Jared said, signaling to the bartender. "And call him a cab."

"I ain't paying for that." O'Malley scowled. "If I took care of every drunk—"

"I'll pay." The man may be a stranger, but his story hit a familiar note in Jared's chest, one he had to heed. He turned to the man, and helped him onto one of the seats, ignoring the nearly overpowering stench of alcohol. "Sir, why don't you sit here a bit? Have some coffee, wait for the cab."

It took a second, then understanding filtered into the older man's bleary gaze. "You're a good man." He patted Jared on the back. "My new best friend. And I don't even know your name."

"Jared Townsend." Jared doubted the man would remember his name in the morning, but it didn't matter. Jared had been down this road often enough to know where it led.

"I'm Sam." His inebriated tongue slurred the "s," and his handshake had a decided wave to it, but the sentiment was there. Jared slid the coffee in front of Sam, and encouraged him to drink up.

The door opened again and Jared swiveled toward the sound, once again grabbing his clipboard and pencil. This time a single woman walked in, but no man followed behind her. Jared's spirits plummeted. Clearly he'd picked the wrong bar. Not a big surprise, given how little experience he had with this kind of scene.

Maybe he should leave, try another place, one with more atmosphere—*some* atmosphere at least—or try a restaurant, a diner, a—

Holy cow. Callie Phillips.

Jared's breath caught, held. The pencil in his hands dropped to the floor, and rolled across the hardwood surface. A woman sang about a broken heart on the jukebox, Sam said something about the quality of the coffee and the tequila toting couple went on fighting, but Jared didn't pay attention. He pushed his glasses up his nose, refocused and made two hundred percent sure.

Yes, it was Callie.

She'd just walked into the bar and upset his perfectly ordered, perfectly balanced life.

Again.

He had the advantage of watching her while her eyes adjusted to the dim interior. He studied her, noting the difference nine years had made. It could have been nine days for all his heart noticed.

She'd cut her hair, and now the dark blond locks

curled around her ears, framed her face, teased at her cheeks. But she still had the same delicate, fine boned face, wide green eyes, and those lips—

Bright crimson lipstick danced across her lips, lips that had always seemed to beg him to kiss them, mesmerized him whenever she talked. He watched her approach, his gaze sweeping over her still lithe curves, outlined in jeans and a bright turquoise top, then returning to her face, to her mouth, and something tightened in his gut.

And Jared Townsend, who never did anything without a reason, a plan, completely forgot why he was here.

CHAPTER TWO

"JARED? Jared Townsend? Is that you? Oh… Wow." She inhaled, her breasts rising with the action, along with Jared's internal temperature. "My goodness. What a…a shock." Callie stopped in front of him, clutching a large box to her chest, her mouth shaped in an O of surprise. "What are you doing here?"

"Uh…" His brain fired, sputtered, fired again. "Research."

She smiled. "Let me guess. You're trying to determine the best beer for forgetting a broken heart?"

"Coors," Sam put in. "Best in sh-sh-show." Then he sent the two of them a wave and headed off to the rest rooms.

Jared glanced down at his icy mug. Beer hadn't helped him get over the broken heart he'd suffered after her, but he kept that ancient history buried, didn't talk about it or drag it out.

Only a masochist dug up a skeleton like that. But damned if his body didn't start playing archaeologist all the same, resurrecting old feelings… and a lot more. There was nothing analytical, statistical or sensible about it. There never had been, not when it came to Callie.

Still, he reminded himself, she had hurt him—and hurt him badly. If he was smart, he'd simply greet her as an old acquaintance and leave it at that.

"I'm here for work," he told her. "Really. Even if it doesn't look it."

Her smile widened. "It doesn't, except for the clipboard, which is so…you." She shrugged, laughed a little, then started to move away. "Well, it was nice to see you again, Jared."

Clipboard was so *him?* Well, damn it, maybe it was, but once upon a time she'd thought of him in a very different way.

Yeah, and how well had that ended up?

He shut off his inner voice. No matter what had happened in the past, a part of Jared wanted Callie to see he had grown and changed. Become a different man. One who wasn't the nerdy professor she had so cavalierly left behind.

A man who could—contrary to his plan five seconds ago—have a conversation with her and be completely unaffected.

Cool with it, even.

"Callie." She pivoted back. "Are you meeting someone here tonight?"

In the space of time it took her to answer, Jared's heartbeat doubled. He caught his breath, waiting. And not because it would make a damned bit of difference to the sheets on his clipboard.

Tonight, he'd stepped into unfamiliar liquor-infused territory to analyze couples, to take that data, feed it into a computer then hand the information over to Wiley Games so they could use it to develop the next generation of couple-oriented games and products. Not exactly the high end research Jared had set out to be doing after he'd received his doctoral degree, but the work at Wiley Games paid the bills and kept him in spreadsheets.

Either way, if there was one particular half of a couple he didn't want to add to his sheaf of papers, it was Callie Phillips.

"No, I'm not meeting anyone, not tonight," she said.

Not an answer that gave him any indication of her status. Single? Attached? No ring adorned her left hand ring finger, so she wasn't married or engaged. What happened? Where was Tony?

"Hey, Callie, what brings you by?" The bartender crossed to them, a friendly smile on his face.

Callie raised the box in her hands. "Your

daughter is now marrying Clarence instead of Clarice."

O'Malley chuckled and took the box from her. "Thank you. Glad you guys caught the mistake before we sent them out. That would have been quite the mess."

"You're more than welcome. The wedding's going to be beautiful."

O'Malley's face softened. "My Jenny, she's an angel. I can't believe she's going to be a bride. Or that I'm old enough to be the father of the bride." He laughed, then thanked her again and moved down to the far end of the bar to refill the other couple's shot glasses.

Callie called a goodbye to O'Malley and turned to go. Before Jared could think about what he was doing—and whether it was a mistake—Jared gestured toward the empty seat beside him. "Would you like to join me?"

What was he doing? Inviting her to stay?

Simple curiosity, that's all it was. Getting caught up on where she'd been all these years.

"I thought you were working," she said.

"It's not busy here, so I'm taking a break." He waved the bartender over to them. "A margarita, on the rocks, with salt."

Callie smiled. "You remembered?"

"I did." He remembered a lot more than just her

favorite drink, but he kept that to himself. Jared reminded himself that he and Callie had broken up for a reason—and staying broken up had been in their best interests.

She took the seat, brushing by him as she did. He inhaled, and with the breath came the light, sweet floral scent of her perfume. "Thanks," she said, when the bartender laid the drink before her.

"No problem, Callie." O'Malley gave Jared another arched brow, this time one of appreciation that the "geek" had a beautiful woman sitting beside him.

Jared tapped the clipboard and grinned. "Nothing's sexier than statistics."

"If you say so, buddy," the bartender said, then headed down to the fighting couple at the other end, who were working on their second set of tequila shots before gearing up for Round Two.

"What kind of research are you doing?" Callie asked.

"Counting the number of beautiful women who come into a bar alone. I'm up to one. I think I should quit while I'm ahead." He grinned. "Actually it's a questionnaire of sorts for couples. A research project for the company I'm working for."

"Sounds exciting."

"It's actually a lot more exciting once you feed

all the information into a computer and start manipulating the data, using it to run statistical probabilities and forecasts. And if I get lucky, hopefully I'll come up with enough data to create some real, hard evidence to bring to a peer-reviewed journal. Something more respectable than the basis of the next 'Twenty Tantalizing Bedroom Teasers.'"

"'Bedroom Teasers'?" Callie chuckled, then raised a dubious brow. "This from the man who dressed up as a biker on Halloween in college? What happened to the leather jacket? The boots? The chaps?"

"Probably shoved in a closet somewhere. I'm strictly a suit and tie guy now. No more of that crazy open road, living by the seat of my pants talk."

His brief, one-night foray into that different persona had been a bad idea. He'd thought that by slipping on a black jacket, climbing on a Harley, he could get Callie to notice him in a way she never had in high school. She had—for a heartbeat—until Tony had stolen her back again, leaving Jared with an extra helmet and a lot of regrets.

No more. He wouldn't journey that road again.

"Pity." Callie took a sip of her drink.

"What's that supposed to mean?"

She shrugged. "You were a lot of fun when you were a…well, not exactly a *bad* boy, but a bad-*ish* boy."

"You make me sound like a five-year-old who wouldn't obey his bedtime."

"If I remember correctly, there wasn't much trouble getting you to bed." Then Callie's face colored and she directed her attention to her drink again.

Jared remembered, too. Remembered too well. One night—a night he'd never forgotten, but she had begged him to never mention again, so that she could marry Tony, with a clear conscience.

Tony—Jared's former best friend. Tony—the man who had stood between them both and been everything Jared wasn't.

And everything Callie wanted.

The memory sucker-punched Jared in the gut and he had to swallow hard before he could breathe again. He'd let Callie go, left college, leaving them behind without a second glance, because he'd thought she was better off—

Had she been? Had he made the right choice?

Hell yes, he had. She would have never been happy with Jared—she'd made that clear. Jared thought that after nine years that last night with Callie wouldn't still sting, would have become some distant memory, fog on his past's horizon.

But nothing about Callie Phillips was foggy in his mind. And he'd be fooling himself if he thought otherwise.

He cleared his throat and took a swig of beer. "So what are you doing now? I take it you're not the bohemian I remember."

She chuckled. "No. I'm now a responsible tax-paying florist."

"A florist?" He assessed her. "That, I can believe. You transformed that hovel I called an apartment into a respectable home, something that didn't scream bachelor dive. You always did have an eye for color and design." Jared straightened his glasses again, then asked the one question that had lingered on the tip of his tongue ever since she'd walked into the bar. Was she still with *him?* "So, how are things with Tony?" he said, nonchal-ant, taking a sip of beer. "Did you guys have any kids?"

"We're divorced. No kids."

Pain flickered in her gaze, and he wanted to ask more, but they'd only been sitting together for five minutes. It wouldn't be right to probe. No matter how curious he was, how the need to know nearly overwhelmed him. What had happened? When had the tarnish appeared on the golden couple? And did Callie ever regret what had happened? Did she ever think about how her leaving Jared had affected him?

Jared took a sip of beer and navigated toward safer subjects. "Do you live here, in the city?"

She nodded. "I settled back in Boston three years ago when Tony got a job in the city. That's when I was hired to be a florist for the Wedding Belles."

"The Wedding Belles?"

"It's a wedding planning company over on Newbury Street. There are six of us, all working for a woman named Belle, hence the name."

"Wow. We're practically neighbors," Jared said. "I live right around the corner from here and the research division of the company I work for is five blocks from Newbury Street."

"All those times we could have run into each other and never did."

"Until now." Jared's gaze met hers. Heat brewed between them, a connection never really lost, even though many years had passed since they'd last seen each other. "Serendipity brings us together again."

"Either that or bad taste in bars." She raised her drink toward his.

"Always the optimist." He smiled, teasing her, then tapped her glass with his own. "You haven't changed, Callie." He paused, and searched her face, looking for the woman he used to know. The one who had made his pulse race, encouraged him to take chances, to think bigger, wilder, to dream of possibilities he'd never dared to have—not until she'd come along. And never dared to have again after she'd gone. "Have you?"

"I should probably go," Callie said suddenly, pushing her margarita to the side. "You have work to do and this…" She looked around the empty bar. "This was not a good idea."

"What do you mean?" She'd just arrived and already she was leaving?

"I just stopped by to drop off the invitations. Thanks for the drink, Jared, and the trip down Memory Lane."

He wasn't going to let her get away that easily. He couldn't, not again. When Callie had been in his life, she'd brought something special, something he'd never found again. Losing her had hurt, hurt like hell. And for just a moment, even though he knew it was crazy and knew she was all wrong for him, he wanted her. "Don't go. Not yet."

"I have a busy day ahead of me tomorrow." She started to slip off the stool, grabbing her clutch purse from the bar.

He reached for her arm, intending only to stop her, to keep her from leaving too soon. But the fire that rocketed through Jared's veins told him that nothing had died between them, at least not on his end. Every bit of the attraction that had been left undone in high school, barely explored in college, lurked under the surface, like tinder simply waiting for that spark.

"Callie—" He cut off the sentence. What ending did he have? He hadn't had a "Cool" transplant in the last nine years, which meant he was still the man he'd always been, the kind of man she hadn't wanted.

Only a fool went for a third strike. Yet, Jared found himself drawn again, wondering if the distance of years would give each of them another shot.

"I should get home," Callie said, stepping out of his grasp. "Nice seeing you again, Jared."

And then she was gone. The door shut behind her, whisking in a cool burst of air as a goodbye.

In an instant, regrets blasted Jared. What the hell was he thinking, letting her get away again? At the very least, he should have asked her out, just to see...

What?

He didn't know, really. They'd been over for a long time—if they'd ever really been anything at all—yet something inside him still wanted to know. Still felt that sense of something undone, that insistent need to complete the storyline.

Why didn't he just leave the past alone—leave her alone?

When he met her gaze, he knew why. Because a part of him still wanted answers to his questions. Wanted to know how Callie felt about those days. Jared didn't want a relationship. He wanted closure.

"Hey, where'd sh-she go? The pretty lady?"

Sam. Jared had forgotten all about him. He turned to find the man, looking a little better with his face washed, and a cup of coffee in him. "She had to leave."

Sam sighed. "The pretty ones always have to go, don't they?"

"Seems that way."

Several people trickled into the bar. None of them Callie. Jared didn't look for couples, no longer cared about his research.

Sam sank onto one of the stools. Jared signaled for a refill of the coffee cup. "My Angie, sh-she's gone now. Lost her, lost my res-sh-tauraunt, lost everything," Sam said. "That's why I'm a...a drunk." He ran a hand through his hair, then shook his head. "My Angie, she'd yell at me, tell me to straighten up. Get it together for the grandkids."

"Why don't you?" Jared asked, his voice almost bitter and angry. As the words left him, he knew the question wasn't just for Sam, but for someone else, someone who wasn't here, and who couldn't answer.

Sam shrugged, then paused for a long moment, staring into the coffee. "Would they really care?"

he asked, his voice low, full of regret. "After all I've done?"

"Yeah," Jared said. "They would."

Sam looked up, the bleariness in his eyes cleared and for a second, he seemed as sober as a minister. "You think we all get second chances, Jared?"

Jared's chest tightened. He hoped so. If his father had lived longer, Jared knew now, with the wisdom of age and experience, that he would have given him a second chance, too. "I'd like to think so."

O'Malley cleared his throat. "Cab's here."

"That's my cue," Sam said, rising. He put out a hand to stop Jared from paying the tab. "I've got it from here. You've done enough. Go after her. Don't wait too long, like me."

Jared watched Sam leave. The words "we all get second chances" rang in his ears. Maybe it was possible.

Jared scrambled off the stool, tossed a few more bills onto the pile for the tip and moved to grab his clipboard. As he picked it up, a germ of an idea sprang to his mind.

What if…he combined a little research with the answers he wanted? What if he found a way to not only peek inside Callie's mind but also use their time together to analyze her reactions? He could do his research—

And find his answers to the past, all at once.

It would solve his problem perfectly. Give him exactly the kind of intimate knowledge his game research needed.

What harm could come of a few days with Callie Phillips? Not a real relationship, just a few dates. After all, Callie hadn't been divorced for very long. Surely she wasn't interested in anything permanent. And neither was he. Once his research was done, he'd be hip deep in work anyway, which meant no time for a life—

Again. Which was what he had done in his last two relationships. Yet, even as he told himself this was the perfect solution for both of them, a tiny bell of doubt rang, telling him things with Callie always had been more complicated than that.

Jared ignored the warning signals and strode out of the bar. Had to be the buzz of beer. Or the part of himself that wasn't interested in signing up for Broken Heart Duty a second time in a decade.

But seeing her, for just a little while—

He couldn't resist that, no matter how much he tried.

He caught up to her a little ways down the sidewalk, her arms wrapped around herself, to ward off the evening chill. He slipped off his jacket and slid it over her shoulders before she could protest.

"Thanks," Callie said. "You were always Sir Galahad."

"That's me. The nerd in waiting." He tipped at his glasses.

"You're not so nerdy, Jared. Just…nice." She smiled. "And that's not so bad, or so easy to find."

Damn, he was tired of her thinking he was nice. Tired of being seen as "just Jared."

Nice guys finished last. And Jared had been left in Tony and Callie's dust.

For one brief moment, she had seen him as something—someone else. Maybe he could give her that peek again. His mind scrambled for a way to connect, to find a path back to who she used to be, to the people they had been nine years ago. And in the process find out what had gone wrong. Why she had found him so lacking and Tony, the heartbreaker, such a better choice.

Then maybe that continual ache would stop hurting.

Music drifted out of O'Malley's bar as the door opened and closed, releasing the fighting couple, who had apparently made up and were now holding hands and snuggling as they left. Other people headed in, the place finally beginning to fill as the night deepened. The music's volume swelled, bass nearly drumming the sidewalk.

Jared took a step forward, and leaned close, his pulse ratcheting up with the nearness of her. "Do you still do that one thing you used to do?"

Her eyebrows arched. "What one thing?"

Jared took another step closer, invading her space now, inhaling her perfume, his research forgotten, his reason for being here long since left by the wayside. "You know what I'm talking about, Mariah Callie."

Callie took in a breath, her chest rising with the movement, and it was all Jared could do not to bend forward and kiss her, just to see if she would still taste as she did. Feel like she used to, her mouth beneath his, her sweet lips against his.

Damn. What kind of game was he playing?

"Yes," she said.

He grinned. "Good. Then let's go do it now."

"You're crazy."

"Maybe," Jared said. "But since when did that ever stop you?"

Callie returned the smile, hers now curving up into one filled with a bit of a dare, a challenge. "Are you sure you can keep up with me?"

Jared leaned forward. His lips brushed against the edge of her hair, nearly kissed the delicate curve of her ear. "Absolutely. I've been practicing."

Callie laughed, the deep, throaty sound Jared remembered, sending his mind roaring down a heady path he thought he'd forgotten. Clearly he hadn't forgotten it. Not at all.

Telling him his plan had one hell of a serious flaw.

CHAPTER THREE

CALLIE hadn't laughed this hard in years. She sat back down at the table in O'Malley's, the bar much more crowded now, clutching her stomach. "Do you really think you had to go that far?"

Jared grinned. His blue eyes captured hers and Callie's pulse quickened. "Absolutely. What's a good Madonna performance without adding in the high-pitched 'oops' at the end?"

"For one, I don't think that's what she says and for another, the whole gyrating thing was more than enough." Callie shook her head, chuckling. "You have to be the worst karaoke singer in the universe. And contrary to what you told me, you have *not* improved since the high school talent show."

"Which is why I have you." He waved a hand in her direction, then at himself. "Baby, you make me look good. You are the Cher to my Sonny."

Callie groaned. "Jared, even your karaoke jokes are bad."

He laughed, then flipped open the menu and slid it her way. "Time for some appetizers. We need fortification if we're going to do the Ike and Tina Turner catalog later."

Callie looked away. Twice, Jared had gone and made references to them as a couple. She hadn't seen the man in nine years and now, wham, it seemed as if they were picking up like a knitter who'd started again on a forgotten afghan.

But wasn't that what her body wanted to do? Heck, every part of her was reacting as if not a moment had passed between the last time she'd seen him and now. Every time he looked at her, every time he smiled, the room seemed to disappear.

And when they'd been on stage, singing together—even though he'd had all the talent of a second-grader in Carnegie Hall—a connection had extended between them, the thread tightening whenever Jared's smile winged Callie's way.

Callie's gaze roamed O'Malley's. The now-busy bartender sent her a friendly thumbs-up, apparently approving of her stage performance, too. Callie waved back, trying to look anywhere but at the man across from her. Maybe if she directed her attention away from Jared, she wouldn't feel so attracted to him.

Behind them, a young man with a blond

Mohawk and a goatee had taken the stage, holding the mike in both hands with a white-knuckled death grip. He stuttered through the first few lines of a Police song, then gave up, to the razzing of a group of drinking buddies in the back corner.

"Poor guy. Probably gearing up for the *American Idol* tryouts, too." Jared shook his head. "Everyone thinks they're a singer."

Callie returned her gaze to Jared. *"Et tú Brute?"*

He laughed. "At least I admit I stink. I'm really only here for moral support for you and for the nachos." He signaled to one of two waiters who were busy juggling the room's tables. "Do you want to order some?" he asked her.

"Nachos are always good, of course." Had he read her mind again? She sat back against her chair, watching as Jared ordered the cheesy chips and some colas for them, impressed for a second time at how much he remembered about her. Nearly a decade had passed since they'd been together and yet, he'd recalled a lot of details. Her favorite drink. Her favorite snack. Her favorite hobby.

When the waiter left, Callie leaned forward. "Okay, what gives? I know you're not some kind of savant, so tell me why you're all over my favorite things. What do you want from me?"

Jared's gaze didn't divert from hers. "Nothing.

Just an evening getting to know you again. Catching up on old times."

"Then how come you remembered everything I love?"

"Is it that hard to think you might have been a memorable person in my life, Callie?"

Silence extended between them, taut, filled with heat, with expectation. He hadn't forgotten her? He'd remembered all those details?

She grabbed the menu again, pretending to study it, which was a lot easier than trying to figure out this odd tension between her and Jared. "I wonder what they have for desserts here."

He tipped the laminated edge downward. "Are you changing the subject?"

"Of course not."

"Then tell me. Have you ever thought about us? About that night? About what might have happened if we—"

"Jared, that's in the past—"

"I meant if we'd gone on tour, of course," he said, his voice shifting into a tease, and Callie wondered if she'd read him wrong, and he didn't mean a relationship "them" at all. Jared reached out and took one of her hands and pulled her out of her chair.

"What are you doing?"

"Do you remember that night, Callie?"

Of course she did. She'd never forgotten that Halloween, that one night in college when she and Jared had stepped over the line from friends and become lovers. One night.

One completely unforgettable night.

Sometimes she wondered what might have happened, had they ended up together, but then her better sense got a hold of her and reminded Callie that happy endings, tied up with a nice neat true love bow, weren't always realistic.

"We sang 'Baby, It's Cold Outside,' and we were terrible," she said, focusing instead on the funny memory of their mangled duet, but then feeling her cheeks heating when she remembered the innuendo in the song, the heat singing it had brewed between them that night. "We were drinking margaritas and probably not thinking entirely straight. I don't know why we even got up on the stage at that college contest."

"We were having fun. A lot of fun."

They had laughed. Laughed so hard, she'd tumbled into his arms outside the bar, seeing Jared in an entirely different light. It had been as if he'd put on that leather jacket, picked up that microphone and become someone else. For the first time, she'd seen him as not a friend, but a man, a very desirable man. When they'd touched, an electricity had erupted between them, bursting into a kiss, a kiss that became more, became everything.

Became an absolutely wonderful, incredible night. Never in her life had Callie ever felt as loved as she had with Jared. He'd made love to her with incredible care, taking his time to treasure her, cherish her.

Love her.

It had been as if he'd memorized her body, knew the sentences of her soul and could finish them with every touch. She'd found herself wondering how she could have missed seeing this side of him, missed this man, and for a moment, considered a future between her and Jared.

But then, in the morning, he'd pulled her into his arms and started talking about where he wanted to go after college. About his plans to buy a house, get married, settle down. Create a forever future.

It had all sounded so fast, nearly chokehold fast, and Callie had panicked and run straight to Tony—the one man who turned out not to be so good at forever.

"Callie?" Jared said, drawing her back to the present. "Are you ready to reprise our greatest hits?"

"Of course." Keep it to music only. Even if the rest of her remembered the details of that night and conveniently kept forgetting the morning after.

"If we're going to do this, then this time," he said, weaving their way past the tables and back toward the small stage at the back of the bar, "I think we need to choose a couple that ended happily. Think Faith Hill and Tim McGraw."

"If *you're* planning on singing, I think we'd be better off with a couple where one of them is a mime," she said, pressing a finger to Jared's lips, knowing this was a crazy idea even as she stepped back onto the stage with him.

Ten songs later, Jared accepted that he would never have a career in music. "There goes my dream of being on the radio. Even O'Malley threatened to buy earplugs on that last one."

Callie laughed and slipped into place beside him as they left the bar. "You clearly have a masochistic urge to embarrass yourself in public."

"It's not so bad as long as I'm in front of total strangers I'll never see again, and as long as you're beside me."

She laughed. "Still playing it safe, huh, Jared?"

"That's me. Safe to a T." He grinned.

"Well, I think you accomplished the total humiliation goal tonight. But you really should have drawn the line at that last pop song."

"That one was purely for your amusement." He caught her eye. "And were you? Amused?"

"Very." The lights above twinkled in her eyes, like stars dancing.

Jared moved closer, unable to maintain his distance another second. All night, she'd enticed him, drawing him closer with every breath, every note. He kept telling himself it was all because he'd missed her, but even Jared knew it was about much, much more. He knew better...and yet, he kept doing the exact opposite of what was smart. "You, on the other hand, were incredible. You can really sing. Why didn't you ever pursue that professionally?"

Callie shrugged, noncommittally. "I don't know. Not my thing, I guess."

"Not your thing? Callie, you are amazing. Seriously. Maybe you should add singing to the wedding business that you're doing."

"Oh, no. The other women don't know I sing at all." She blushed and turned away. "No one knows."

For some reason, it thrilled Jared that he knew. That she'd shared this with him, and no one else. "So you're a closet karaoke-er?"

She laughed. "Yeah, I guess you could say that."

He reached up and cupped her jaw, finally touching the face he'd been dying to feel all night. Her skin was satin against his palm, her delicate features cast by the soft evening light. He moved closer, closing the gap between them, the night providing its soft, quiet blanket of intimacy. "Seems a shame," Jared said. "To have a gift and keep it wrapped up so tight."

"Jared, it's complicated."

"If I remember right, everything with you was complicated."

She lifted her chin, so close he could kiss her with nothing more than a whisper of effort. He shouldn't. He needed to maintain his distance. His professionalism, the research. That's what he told himself he'd come here for, not a relationship with the woman who had always been the complete opposite of him, who'd broken his heart, left the shards in her wake when she'd run off with his best friend.

But she was smiling and he kept having trouble remembering any of that.

"If I remember right," Callie said, "that was part of what you liked about me…and part of what drove you crazy."

"That wasn't all that drove me crazy," he murmured.

A heartbeat passed between them. Another, and all Jared could see, hear, think about, was the movement of her crimson lips, the sound of her breath. Her mouth opened again, lips parted ever so slightly, like an invitation.

And Jared dipped down, so close his lips could almost brush against hers. Desire drummed hard in his veins.

Then common sense sent an icy shower of reality across his senses and Jared drew back, his gaze lingering on hers for one long moment before he released her. "Now that we're all grown up, it seems you're not the only one who can make things complicated."

CHAPTER FOUR

IF THERE had ever been a time when Callie wished she had better bluffing skills, it was the next night at the monthly poker game for the Wedding Belles. "So, Callie, how'd it go at O'Malley's?" Audra asked. "Did you stick to your resolution and not meet a man?"

Callie dipped her head, avoiding Audra's inquisitive gaze. "Of course not."

She'd run into an old friend. That didn't technically make it meeting a man.

The heat on Callie's neck told her the entire assemblage of women was staring at her. So much for bluffing. "So, shall we get back to the card game?" Callie asked, picking up her pile of five cards and fanning them out in her hand.

"Are you going to tell us his name?" Audra asked. She shifted her slender body in the kitchen chair, her blue eyes wide with suspicion.

"Whose name?"

"This man who has you blushing like a teenager with her first crush."

Regina O'Ryan, the company photographer, chuckled, then dipped her head to look at her poker hand. Her brown hair swung forward, the locks curving around her heart-shaped face. "Audra, maybe Callie wants to keep him a secret."

"No secrets. I just want to play cards."

"Uh-huh," Audra said, not believing her for a second.

Callie rolled her eyes at Audra's persistence, then glanced down at her cards. Two jacks, an ace, a three and a four. She slipped the three and the four out, laid them facedown on the table and slid them over to Audra, who, as the hostess, was also the dealer for the monthly ladies' poker game.

The Wedding Belles played for pocket change because they looked forward to the camaraderie and the margaritas more than anything else.

Only four of the six Belles sat in Audra's sunflower-yellow kitchen today, two-thirds of the hardworking, dynamic team. Natalie Thompson was busy teaching a cake decorating class to high school students in downtown Boston; Julie Montgomery was running some last-minute errands. Belle was closing up the shop.

"Audra, I think you might be onto something. Callie does seem awfully evasive." Regina picked up her cards, but didn't glance at her hand.

"That's because she doesn't believe Mr. Right exists," Audra said, rising to refill the chip bowl.

"Are you serious?" Serena asked. Serena, the wedding dress designer, was the biggest Prince Charming proponent in the group. "You have to believe in Mr. Right. It's like a job requirement to be a wedding planner."

"Exactly," Regina agreed. "How many weddings have you helped put together in the three years you've been working here, Callie? Dozens and dozens, right?" Regina finally decided on her poker hand, and slipped Audra a card for exchange. "Our clients sure seem to find good guys and plenty of great picks."

Callie scoffed. "So do the bargain shoppers who shove you out of the way at the annual Filene's Basement wedding gown sale."

"I still have a bruise from the last one," Serena added. "Those women are vicious."

Regina chuckled. "Seriously. We're in the business of creating dream weddings. We're *supposed* to believe in true love and happy endings."

"She has a point, Callie." Audra handed Regina a card from the deck. Regina smiled. Audra eyed her friend, weighing her expression. As the

Wedding Belles financial guru, if anyone could spot someone bluffing about their money, it was Audra. "What do you have there, Regina? Anything good?"

"Of course not." Regina's voice raised a couple octaves. The company's photographer might be great at taking pictures, but most of them could call her on her bluffs. "And I'd never tell you if I did. How about you, Callie? You planning on trying out for the Texas Hold 'Em competitions?"

"You all know how bad I am at bluffing." Callie took a sip of her frosty margarita, the cold drink a perfect accompaniment to the chips and dip Audra had set out for an appetizer. "Plus, I usually attract low cards like dogs attract fleas."

Regina laughed. "Maybe that's what we all need. A Labrador. All you have to do is feed him and he's not only loyal for life, he never asks for the remote."

"Seriously, I don't think you should give up on love or men," Audra added. "I mean, we all need to have hope, don't you agree? I don't care what the statistics say, I believe in happy endings. It's just not logical to assume Mr. Right doesn't exist. Especially when we watch all these clients walk down the aisle and know we helped create that perfect moment. Mr. Right is out there, I'm sure of it, especially since I'm planning my own wedding to him right now." Audra took a sip from her drink. "Besides, we've all met more than our share of Mr. Wrongs—"

"Absolutely. Look at me. I've got a Mr. Pretty-Sure-He's-Right," Serena James piped in. The bubbly blond dress designer was currently in a long-term relationship, and a huge champion for the opinion that there was a Mr. Right out there for everyone.

"I used to think that, too," Callie said. "But then I met Tony."

"One bad apple doesn't spoil the whole harvest," Serena said. "What was wrong with the man you met last night?"

"Nothing." Callie sighed. "Everything. He used to be Tony's best friend."

"Oh," Regina said, then realization dawned further. "*Oh.*"

"It means there's history between us," Callie said, plucking a chip from the bowl.

"No, it means you're not starting from scratch," Serena said.

"I'm not starting anything," Callie insisted. Though a part of her wondered where things might have gone if Jared had kissed her. Would they have started something—

Something they had begun, but left undone all those years ago?

"Would finding true love be so bad?" Audra asked.

"No, not at all," Callie replied. "I just think it's not realistic to think all of us end up happy."

"Why not?" Serena asked. "Look at the odds. I have a great guy. Audra's engaged. Regina's married."

"And don't forget Julie," Regina said. "She's found a great guy in Matt."

Serena sighed. "They are *so* cute together. I think it's kinda sad, though, that they're just planning to go down to city hall. Julie's been working for us since day one. She deserves the kind of weddings she plans."

"I agree," Callie said, glad for the change of subject away from her own life, and for the focus on someone who truly needed a happy ending.

Julie, the Belles assistant, had been hit financially from left and right, both from her own personal life and from her fiancé Matt's business struggles. After Matt's custom plane building business lost a huge account, Julie and Matt had decided to pour their entire wedding savings into the company, in order to save everyone's jobs. Things were still rocky at his business, but they were on the upswing.

Julie and Matt were good people, who'd simply hit a financial road bump.

Callie might not believe in true love for herself,

but she was happy to see Julie had found a wonderful man. If anyone deserved a happy ending, Julie did.

"Those hospital bills from her mom and that flood in her house last spring..." Callie's voice trailed off in sympathy. Hard times had slammed her before, too, and she'd been battered by the twin winds of financial and personal pressures. She'd gone through both during her marriage to Tony, who hadn't been much for holding down a job—or remembering a word of what he'd promised during the wedding ceremony. "Julie said it was too much and she and Matt need to save every penny they have, until his business is finally on its feet."

"And then, they can have kids," Serena said with a dreamy sigh. Serena, always the one who had dreams for the future, the one with the vision. "Julie's been eager to start a family and would make such a great mom."

"She definitely would." Regina beamed, the photographer's generous smile taking over her face.

Callie and Tony had never had children. A blessing, her mother had said, when the judge finalized the divorce decree. But to Callie, it had been the final ironic twist in her life story. The woman who had never put down roots, who'd married a man who couldn't sit still, had been left with nothing more to show for all those years than a piece of paper and a few sticks of furniture. Not exactly a monument to achievement.

"Every woman deserves a wonderful wedding," Serena said, glancing down at her hand, then her pile of coins, clearly agonizing over whether to bet on the cards she'd been dealt. "I wish we could do something for Julie to help her out."

"Of course there is something." Audra brightened and laid her cards facedown on the table. "We're the Wedding Belles. Why don't we throw Julie and Matt a wedding? I'm sure Belle would be all over it. She's such a romantic. Natalie would make a killer cake. If all of us worked on it and contributed our amazing skills—" she grinned at her friends "—we'd be able to pull this off."

"That's a great idea," Callie said, warmth spreading through her heart for these women, her friends, who had been with her through the trauma of her divorce. Always ready with a hug, a sympathetic ear, or a simple chocolate bar left on her worktable. What would she have done without them?

They were the best friends Callie could have imagined. Better that than some fairy tale concocted by a couple of brothers. What kind of happy endings could two guys with a last name of Grimm create anyway?

Serena put her cards down, her eyes bright with excitement, the wheels of dress designs clearly turning in her head. "I can already imagine the dress I'd like to create for Julie. She'll look like an angel."

"And I'll take black and white photos of the wedding," Regina added, the sense of energy soaring through the group. Callie felt it, as surely as a breeze. This was the energy that comprised the Belles, that gave every one of their weddings its unique flavor. "Julie saw some in my portfolio and loved them."

"I can just see it," Audra said. "What about you, Callie?"

Callie nodded, already picturing the kind of bouquets and arrangements she'd design. "I can imagine it, too. If there's one thing I can always see, it's someone else's wedding." She smiled. "Julie loves gardenias. I'll make sure she has flowers that would make the Dutch drool."

"Good. It's settled. We'll give Julie and Matt a wedding they won't forget. And we'll make it a huge surprise." Audra smiled, then picked up her cards again. "She's going to be so thrilled."

"She already is. Matt's a dream. I think Julie got the last Mr. Right on earth," Callie said, truly happy for her friend. She didn't envy Julie's happiness a bit. But there were days, especially after she'd watched one more couple ride off into a sunset full of happiness and promises, when she wondered if maybe there would ever be a little of that for her, too.

Callie shook her head, dismissing the blue funk. Dwelling on the disaster that had been her marriage did nothing but stir a pot best left alone.

She picked up her new cards and slipped them into her hand. A jack and an ace. Full house. Maybe her luck was looking up—at least poker-wise. She tossed two dimes into the center pile.

"Ooh, Callie's betting high," Regina said, matching the bet. "Must be a good hand."

"I'm out," Serena said, folding her cards and laying them on the table. "I've got nothing."

Audra's deep blue gaze met Callie's. For a second, she measured what she saw in her friend's eyes, then threw in two dimes. "I'll meet your twenty cents. And raise you a quarter." She tossed in the silver coin.

"Too rich for my blood," Regina said, laughing and setting her pile of cards aside. "Especially when all I have is a pair of twos."

"I'll match your quarter and call." Callie moved to add another coin to the pile.

Audra reached out and put a hand over Callie's. "Wait. Let's up the ante a bit."

"Up the ante? But we always bet pocket change."

"I mean something more interesting. We are, after all, the Wedding Belles. We're supposed to believe in happily ever after, but you don't, Callie, and I happen to think you're wrong. If we're going to pull off this wedding for Julie and Matt, then I think you should test your theory about there not being enough Mr. Rights in the world to go around. If you win, then we'll put on Julie's wedding, congratulate her for getting the last great guy and resign ourselves to the fact that there aren't any other Mr. Rights left, but if I win…"

Callie narrowed her gaze. "If you win…what?"

"Then you have to go along with an experiment. A challenge." Audra smiled. "Because I happen to think you're wrong. I mean, I work on weddings all day and I'm engaged myself. If I don't believe in Mr. Right, then I should go into a different field."

"Yeah, funeral planning," Regina interjected. The four of them burst out laughing.

"It would be nice if you were right, Audra." Callie thought of Jared. He'd awakened something in her last night, something that had lain dormant in her for years. Could Audra be right or was Callie merely wishing on an impossible star? "It's been a long, dry spell, girls, and I could use a guy who doesn't shred my heart like a Ginsu knife."

"Or one who doesn't look like a guilty puppy every time he looks my way," Regina muttered.

"Everything okay with Dell, Regina?" Audra asked.

"Oh, yeah, just fine." Regina let out a laugh. "I'm kidding, that's all."

For a second Callie wondered if everything wasn't as perfect as Regina was leading them to believe. She scanned her friend's face, but the shadow had passed and Regina's regular sunny countenance had returned. Perhaps Callie had imagined it.

"So, Callie, are you game?" Audra asked. "For an experiment if you lose?"

At first, Callie opened her mouth to protest, but then the whisper of a challenge tickled at her. It raced through her blood, sending a shiver of excitement, of possibilities, down her spine. When had she last felt like that? Excited about her future?

Last night with Jared had reawakened the Callie she used to be. When they'd sung together, he'd reminded her of the woman she'd been in college.

And when he'd leaned down, his breath warm on hers, a kiss only a whisper away, he'd made her heart race in a way it hadn't raced in…forever.

Like it had when she'd been the girl who had dropped everything at a moment's notice to jet off for an adventure. The woman who had taken the detours, tried a new city, a different town. She'd

SHIRLEY JUMP 57

done almost anything once, playing a game of spontaneity with every single day.

She'd lost that Callie somewhere in her marriage, buried her under a lot of disappointments and hurts. Did she still exist?

And if she found that woman, would returning to who she used to be ruin Callie's carefully built life?

A crazy thought, she told herself. Surely she could take on this simple little bet from Audra. Maybe this was exactly what Callie needed to get out of this emotional funk she'd been in since the divorce and start moving forward.

She folded her cards together and leaned forward, excitement increasing her pulse. "What kind of challenge are you talking about? Exactly?"

"One where we see if your theory holds up in the real world. Meaning, you get back in the dating game and see if Mr. Right doesn't just pop up."

"Yeah, from underneath a rock," Regina put in with a chuckle.

"Girls, this is just penny poker," Serena said, putting a hand of caution over the pot of change in the center of the table. "We never bet anything real. It's just for fun."

Audra's eyes glittered and a smile crossed her face. "This could be fun, too. And besides, Callie, it's about time you jumped into the deep end."

Her grin widened and a tease edged her words. "Come on in the dating pool. The water's warm, and with some guys, really hot. And who knows? You might find true love in the process."

"What exactly are we betting here, Audra?" Callie asked.

"You take a chance with this Jared—" Audra put up a finger "—and don't try to pretend he didn't affect you because it's all over your face."

"Take a chance?"

"Go out with him again, if you lose this hand, on a *real* date. And see where it goes."

See where things went with Jared? Callie had already done that years ago. And yet…

Hadn't that almost-kiss between them been on her mind nonstop since last night? Didn't a part of her wonder what might have happened if he had kissed her? Or if she had closed the gap?

It had been eighteen months since Callie's divorce. Eighteen months spent rehashing her marriage, trying to figure out where things had gone wrong. Fourteen months of going over every conversation, every argument. But not of dating seriously.

What was that theory about hitting your thumb? Something about quit doing it if it hurts. Well, Callie had quit men. Because they hurt her heart.

Audra waited across from her, a friendly challenge on her face. Callie thought of the full house she held in her five cards. One of the best hands she'd had in months. Surely Audra didn't hold anything better. And then, they could all drop this crazy idea. She and Jared weren't right for each other. He was the practical, suburbs kind of guy and she was the wild one who'd never been able to stay in one place for long.

Either way, there was almost no chance Audra's cards could beat Callie's. The whole issue was probably moot.

"Yeah, I'm game," Callie said. "I call. Let's see what you've got."

Callie fanned out her cards, splaying them proudly across the laminate surface of Audra's kitchen table. Three jacks, two red, one black, paired with two red aces.

She watched Audra do the same. One red card—a six. Another—a seven. A third—an eight. A fourth—a nine.

When the fifth red card—a ten—appeared, Callie knew she'd just been roped into dating Jared again by a straight flush. In hearts, no less.

CHAPTER FIVE

BELLE'S eagle eye didn't miss a thing, either.

"Did you meet a man at O'Malley's the other night, darlin'?" Belle asked the second Callie walked into work the next morning.

Callie avoided her boss's inquisitive gaze by flipping through a stack of mail. "Are you all in on some big conspiracy?" Callie laughed. "He was an old friend, nothing more."

"Uh-huh," Belle said, the lilt in her Southern accent making it clear she didn't believe Callie one bit and already heard it all from the other women. "Well, when this man you *didn't* meet calls again looking for you, what should I tell him?"

"He called here?"

Belle laughed and settled her ample frame onto the settee in the reception area. On a small table beside her sat a bouquet of white roses, a daily arrangement Callie made for Belle, a tribute to Belle's late and much loved first husband Matthew.

"He called twice. Wanted to know what time you came in and if you had time for lunch. That boy sounded positively smitten to me."

Callie bit back the smile that threatened to take over her face. Already she was smiling about Jared's call? Oh, this was so not a good sign. "What did you tell him?"

"I said I'm not your social secretary, honey, but he's welcome to call back after ten and find out for himself. Make him do a little work and he'll appreciate the chase all that much more." Belle laughed.

"After ten?" Callie glanced at the clock. "Why so late?"

"My, my, that man does have you off your game today. Did you forget that Marsha Schumacher is coming in at nine to discuss the flowers for her wedding?"

Callie groaned. "Oh, no. I did. Is she bringing her mother?"

"Doesn't she always? I can stay, darlin'. Run some interference, block any unwanted matriarchal meddlin'. I've been married a few times. I know how to handle meddlin'."

Callie laughed. "I'll be fine, Belle. But thank you."

"Hey, I'm here for you, honey, anytime you need me." Belle rose and came around the coffee table to Callie's side. "And I mean that about more than just Marsha."

"I know."

Belle drew Callie into a hug. "Oh, darlin', your sunshine brightened my days after my last husband died. And I'm just so proud of the Callie you've become since I met you."

The world Callie had lived in before existed light years away from the cheery, tulle-filled world of Wedding Belles. A hundred times over, Callie had been grateful for Belle, who'd brought her under her ample wing, and given her not just a regular, stable job, but a voice of wisdom and love. When she met Belle, Callie felt as if she'd finally be able to escape the weeds and settle in among the daisies, become one herself. Though there were days when Callie wondered if she really fit in here. Maybe…

She shook off the thought. She was happy. A little desire to travel was nothing more than that.

"I'm a lot different from that wild woman," she said.

"You are, indeed." Belle laughed. "You've circled around like a cat who's found a new end to her tail."

Callie echoed Belle's laughter. "You are one of a kind, Belle. You and your sayings."

"That's what I told all my husbands." She winked, then headed out the door, just as Marsha and Barbara Schumacher whisked inside, early for their appointment.

Marsha had clad herself head to toe in her favorite color—pink. From her pink sweater to her pink skirt, a pink faux fur coat and even, Lord help her, pink boots. Barbara had opted for real fur, a dark brown mink, which made her daughter look all the more like a piece of cotton candy.

The Schumachers weren't bossy, just…needy. They reminded Callie of her own mother, who made marrying often a sport. Her mother, however, hadn't accompanied marrying often with marrying well, and was usually divorced as quickly as she was remarried. This morning, her mother had called—again—to announce another impending breakup, one where she was expecting her daughter to offer emotional support.

Callie hadn't had time to do much more than listen before her mother had said she had to go, off to play golf at a singles' event. "On the hunt again," her mother said, laughing, the conversation over before it really began. Par for the mother-daughter relationship course.

Barbara Schumacher clutched a sleeping Pomeranian in her arms like a prize from Ed McMahon. Maybe Callie should stop at a pet store on the way home, get her mother a portable dog. It would at least give Vanessa something else to focus on besides finding her next fiancé.

"Oh, Callie, I can't wait to see my flowers!"

Marsha rushed forward. "Do you have my designs ready?"

"Absolutely," Callie said, greeting both bride and mother and leading them toward the French doors connecting to a dining room adjacent to the main reception room. The Belles used the area as a way to showcase tablescapes, linens and flowers, giving brides a visual preview of their wedding designs.

"The florist *should* have the designs ready," Barbara said to her daughter, giving the little dog a pat on the head. The Pomeranian roused, then went back to sleep. "That's what you expected, baby, and you should always get what you expect. And then some."

"Last week, we talked about something tall to really wow your guests, yet make the most of your spring theme," Callie said, ignoring the mother of the bride's barb. "Tell me what you think of this." With a flourish, she opened the doors, revealing the grand display she'd set up at the end of the day yesterday.

"Oh, those are *beautiful!*" Marsha exclaimed, dashing forward, one hand over her mouth. She reached out and fingered a lily petal, gently, as if it were crystal, then stepped back to admire the towering topiary arrangement of stargazer lilies, Gerbera daisies, godetia and calla lilies springing out of a thin, twenty-inch-high silver fluted vase. Ming fern and bear grass provided a touch of greenery and soft accent to the bright color, while delicate English ivy trailed like fingers to the table. "But…do you think it's pink enough?"

"It's very pink," Callie replied, thinking that if she'd used any more colored flowers, the whole thing would look like a bottle of indigestion medicine.

Marsha tapped her lip, thinking. "Maybe we should sprinkle the whole thing with, like, pinkish gold dust. I saw that once on one of those craft shows and oh—" she pressed a hand to her chest "—it was like it had been kissed by pink angels. I loved it."

"Oh, baby," Barbara said. "If that's what you want, we'll do just that. Angel kisses for my angel."

Callie forced herself not to cringe. "I really don't think that would add to the arrangement. It might…ah, overpower and detract from the surrounding beauty. I'd hate to see anything steal attention away from the bride." Callie smiled at Marsha.

"That's true. I wouldn't want that. Well, maybe we could throw in some pink carnations or other pink flowers. Or—" Marsha got so excited by her idea she nearly jumped up and down "—we could glue little pink bows all over the flowers and then on the vase and then we could scatter them all over the table and—"

Callie groaned inwardly. Her mind flitted to Jared, imagining how he'd react to such an illogical, over the top feminine proposition. "How about we keep it simple, elegant, like your dress?"

"How would you do that?"

"We could drape a pink tablecloth over the white tablecloth that you were going to have. That would add an extra layer of your favorite color." Again, Callie thought of Jared, picturing his reaction to the entire hilarious scene of arguing over pink fairy dust and pink bows, while a sleepy Pomeranian looked on, letting out little yawns from time to time. She shook off the thoughts.

Focus on work. Not him. Especially not him. Jeez, get her on the stage for a few songs with the guy and suddenly she became as infatuated as a teenager at a pop concert. Maybe she needed more sleep. Or maybe she was just in serious pink overload.

"Could it be the exact same pink as my bridesmaids' dresses and the ties and cummerbunds?" Marsha asked.

"Oh, Marsha," her mother said, "you always have the most creative ideas. Why, if you had the time, you could have designed this whole wedding yourself."

"I could have, couldn't I? It's too bad we couldn't have found a way to make the cotton candy favors I wanted." Marsha pouted and sent a look Callie's way as if it were all her fault she couldn't produce a way to make miniature printable cotton candy figurines.

"I think that pink color will certainly be doable," Callie said, hoping that concession would soothe her bride, and also get her own mind back on the Schumacher wedding. Thank goodness ninety percent of the Belles brides were a whole lot easier to work with. She picked up her pen. "Now, back to the flowers. For the boutonnieres and the corsages…"

She began to work down the list of floral arrangements with Marsha, trying to talk the bride out of one pink addition after another, her mother chiming in about price and her baby's desires. Marsha was a likable client, but one with an incredible fixation on that single color. Her mother and Serena had thankfully talked her out of the hot-pink wedding dress, and Marsha's fiancé had firmly put his foot down about wearing a pink tuxedo. He'd pulled the Belles aside during the first meeting and begged them to keep his bride-to-be's pink passion to a minimum, if only to make the wedding palatable to the male guests.

But all the while Callie was dealing with

Marsha, her gaze kept straying away from the flowers and toward the clock. Nine-fifteen, nine-thirty, nine-forty-five. The phone rang from time to time, and Callie would excuse herself from Marsha's incessant debate over fuchsia versus pale cherry to answer the calls, but every time it was someone other than Jared.

After Callie hung up, she'd berate herself for even being disappointed that she'd been waiting for Jared to call in the first place.

He was part of her past—a past she'd worked hard to put behind her—and that's where he should stay.

Uh-huh. If that were so, then why did she keep mentally replaying the other night? The way a much more adult Jared had sent her hormones raging in ways she hadn't even imagined all those years ago?

She reminded herself that she and Jared had had one brief ill-timed night together. Then Tony had come back, begging her for one more chance, and any thoughts of any kind of relationship with Jared Townsend had been washed away as easily as sand on a beach.

Yeah, and look where that choice got you, her mind whispered. Still, she'd do her best to forget Jared. To forget the past.

But when the phone rang again at nine-fifty-five, Callie nearly lunged for the receiver, thankful that Marsha had just left and she didn't have the added distraction of the client. "Wedding Belles, this is Callie speaking."

"Is this the woman who can make magic with magnolias and bring a man to his knees with a song?"

Jared's voice. Everything inside of Callie roared to life, awakened again, as if it had lain dormant all these years. She laughed. "It is. And is this the man who can turn spreadsheets into works of art?"

"Data DaVinci, that's me." He chuckled. "What are you doing for lunch today?"

"I, ah, have an appointment." Bet or no bet, he was a friend, always had been. She should keep it that way, if she were smart. Keep her past where it was, because if she got caught up in that old Callie—

"That's not what I heard. Your boss said your schedule is free from twelve to two."

Belle. Matchmaking again. That woman would manufacture a happy ending if she couldn't find one. Probably working in concert with the other Belles. Callie immediately swore off the monthly poker games. "Jared, the other night was fun, but—"

"Stop. What's so wrong with a little fun? Because I know that's one thing I could use more of. What's happened to you, Callie?"

"Nothing."

"Really? Because the Callie I remember would have found any excuse to live it up a little."

She closed her eyes and pinched the bridge of her nose. "I'm not like that anymore. I don't take risks." Yet even as she said the words, the old urge to do just that tugged at her.

Hadn't her friends encouraged her to do just that? Told her to get out of her rut, providing a little impetus with that bet? Maybe they'd seen something she'd missed.

Maybe they were right.

"Jared—"

"I'll see you at twelve." Then he hung up, cutting off her objections.

Callie held the phone in her hand for a long time, staring at it and wondering what she had just gotten herself into. Jared seemed determined to bring back the very past she'd done so much work to escape.

A past that still whispered at the fringes of her mind, with a familiar tune of wanderlust. She was happy here, she reminded herself. Happy with her job. Her friends. Her life.

But still…some days, it seemed as if a piece of the puzzle had been dropped on the floor, left behind in a closet. She'd get this overwhelming urge to leave, go find the piece, fill in that one personal gap that had always seemed open.

And that, Callie knew, was what scared her because it led her to make impetuous decisions, the kind she'd made with Tony.

She shrugged off the worries. It was all hormones or something. Nothing more.

"The telephone won't bite, you know."

Callie turned to find Natalie standing in the doorway, a bemused smile on the cake decorator's face, her blond hair in its perpetually mussed bun on top of her head. Callie laughed and replaced the receiver in the cradle. "Sorry. Just thinking."

"What about?" Natalie started walking toward the kitchen, a load of bags from the local decorating supply store in her arms. Callie took two of them and followed along, helping Natalie unload the cake decorations she'd bought. Miniature brides and grooms, little Grecian pillars, edible pearls, luster dust, cake boards and decorating foil all went into the various cabinet drawers and shelves that organized Natalie's small kitchen area.

"I'll give you three guesses."

Natalie turned to Callie and grinned, her fist on her hip. "Given the look on your face, I only need one. A guy."

"I must have man trouble written all over my forehead today. Either that or you and Belle have suddenly become psychic."

Natalie poured each of them a cup of coffee, then handed one of the mugs to Callie. "Nope. Audra, Regina and the others have just been talking. You didn't think they'd keep that bet to themselves, did you?"

Callie groaned. "Is everyone in this business invested in my romantic future?"

Natalie's hand covered Callie's, the touch of a longtime friend, one who had weathered a difficult path of her own, but one with a far more tragic ending after her husband had died in a motorcycle accident, leaving her with eight-year-old twins. Still, the petite woman maintained her sunny perspective and kept the mood light and the sweets abundant at the Wedding Belles. "Yeah, we are. It comes with the deluxe friend package."

Callie chuckled. "You guys are the best."

"That's why we're the Belles." Natalie turned to the refrigerator and withdrew a sliver of cake. "Here, you need to taste this one. Tell me what you think."

"Nat, I really think this whole part of your job is a shame. What kind of cake maker is a diabetic?" Callie bit into the cake and nearly moaned at the white chocolate cake with raspberry filling that hit her palate with a burst of flavor. "Oh, this is your best."

Natalie grinned. "I thought you said my devil's food cake was my best."

Callie laughed, then scooped up another bite. "So you have two bests. You're an incredible baker, what can I say?"

"Speaking of which, I have an appointment with a client in a couple hours, so I better get some more samples prepared. And don't forget, we have a group meeting for the Cross wedding at two."

Callie nodded. The day would be a long one, as all the spring days were. From April to June spelled wedding season, which meant they'd be working late hours for months. "I'll be here. I have some preliminary designs already worked up that I think Alicia will like and I'll pull together a sample cascading bouquet with those Dendrobium orchids she said she wanted, too."

"Great. See you then." Natalie grabbed her purse off the counter, then paused before she left. "Oh, and enjoy your lunch date."

"Does everyone around here know everything about my love life?"

Natalie laughed. "Of course. That's our job. And your job is to go out on that date, like you agreed."

Callie threw up her hands. "I'm beaten at—"

"—your own game," Natalie finished with a laugh. "And when it comes time to plan *your* wedding, we'll be even more on top of every little detail."

Callie put up her hands, warding off the possibility. "Trust me, we're a long, long, *long* way from that day."

"Uh-huh. That's what they all say." Natalie gave her a grin. "Okay, now I really have to get out of here. And remind me not to bring my kids around here for the next couple of weeks."

"Why not?"

"I saw a sign for free puppies across the street. If my twins see that, they'll be begging me for a puppy. And worse, one *each*." Natalie shuddered. "That's all I need is twins *and* twin puppies." She laughed, then headed out the door.

Callie chuckled, then got to work busying herself with paperwork—completing orders, sketching out some designs and following up with clients—for the next two hours. The hall clock gonged twelve, at the same time that the bell over the front door pealed, announcing a visitor.

But Callie knew—she knew, without even looking up—that this wasn't a client, a delivery, or anyone else but Jared.

She felt his presence as surely as she could a spring breeze, a shift in temperature, a whisper in her ear. Callie paused in the words she was writing and looked up, her gaze meeting his in an instant.

"So," he said, that familiar grin on his face, "what are you in the mood for?"

You.

When he smiled at her like that, she forgot exactly why she objected to dating him. What reason she had against seeing him. And thought about nothing that had to do with food and everything to do with being with him the night before.

"Italian," Callie said, deciding she better darn well get decisive and get there quick. She'd go with him to lunch, tell him that seeing each other on any kind of romantic basis was crazy, despite the bet.

They were polar opposites, with completely different goals in life, and better off, as always, as just friends. Weren't they?

"Good thing I made reservations at Café Donatello." He grinned.

"Pretty confident in my food choice?"

He gave her a cocky smile. "I'm confident about a lot of things."

"That's one thing we have in common."

"Back in high school and college, you used to think we were as different as pencils and fireworks."

"Well, personality wise, sure. But we have things in common."

"Like what?"

"Well, you…" Her voice trailed off. Why was he putting her on the spot like that? And why had he taken a step closer? Every time he did that, she stopped thinking. "You like…singing, and well, so do I."

Oh, smooth answer, Callie. Way to go.

A grin quirked up one side of his face. "All these years and you still don't know me that well, do you? But I know you, Callie. Better than you think." Then Jared moved back, his smile lightening, and he gestured toward the door. "Right now, though, all we're talking about is lunch, right? Ready to go?"

"Uh, yeah." Callie grabbed her purse and followed him out the door. But as she and Jared walked down the street and around the corner to the exclusive Café Donatello, she had to wonder again why he had kept track of a friend from high school, a momentary relationship in college.

Had he cared more than she'd realized? If that had been so, then why hadn't he ever said anything?

A warm spring breeze played at the ends of Callie's hair, tickling up her neck, whispering along her skin. She caught the scent of blooming daffodils, tulips, the dawn of the new season. Spring ushered in that sense of hope, of a renewed beginning, and Callie caught herself glancing at Jared and wondering…

What if.

What if she hadn't run off on that crazy whim

and eloped with Tony? What if she'd woken up that morning and gotten swept up in Jared's talk of forever and white picket fences? What if he'd taken her along that road?

Where would she be today? How would her life be different?

But Jared hadn't done that. He'd talked about those dreams, then turned to Callie and read her like a book. *"But that's not the kind of life you want, is it, Callie?"*

In those words, she'd known his four-bedroom dreams weren't meant to include her. And why should they have? Hadn't she made it clear a hundred times over that she wasn't the settling down kind?

But for a moment there, she had thought of settling down with him. And when he'd said that, it had hurt.

"You're awfully deep in thought," Jared said. "Pondering rose and carnation issues?"

She laughed. "No. Something…deeper."

Jared slipped her hand into his. "Like what?"

"To be honest, why you never married." She felt the tension in his touch, telling her she'd touched on a nerve. "Why are you still single all these years later, Jared?"

"To be honest, I don't have time, or room, for anything serious." A couple brushed by them, linked arm in arm, as if bucking that notion. "As soon as this research project is done, I'll be buried in the development phase and I won't have time to do much more than grab some crackers for dinner and wave at my pillow at night."

"You? But I remember you as being Mr. Serious. The man who was going to settle down. Have the house and the minivan and the kids."

He glanced away. "It didn't work out that way."

"Why?" She knew she shouldn't push, should let it be. It was none of her business, after all, but still she cared. This was Jared, after all.

"My life got in the way. Other…aspects of it."

Callie nearly laughed. If anything summed up Jared, that sentence did. All words and less emotion, less getting to the heart of things. That had always been the biggest problem with him—she never knew how he felt, because he kept putting his intellect in the way. He kept so much of him to himself.

"I'm surprised you of all people did get married," he said. "Callie Phillips, the woman who lived on a wing and a prayer."

"It was a whim. One of those, 'Why not?' kind of things," she said. "And after we did it—" she rolled her eyes "—we should have said, 'Why did we?'"

"Marriage wasn't what you expected?"

"Let's just say marriage and I were not a good

mix. Tony and I never had the traditional married life anyway. We never stayed in one place, never really settled down. We moved more times than most people go to the grocery store."

"And you liked that kind of life?"

She shrugged. "Sure. Life is an adventure, right?"

They circumvented two mothers chatting on the sidewalk while their babies slept in strollers. "But you're here now and you've lived in Boston for three years. That's called settling down in my book," Jared said.

"I like it here. I like my job, my friends."

"So is this something permanent?"

Permanent. That word did not exist in Callie's vocabulary. "I don't like to think about anything in permanent terms."

"You mean you're just looking for temporary relationships? Nothing deep? Meaningful? Lasting?"

Put like that, it sounded so...crass. So cold.

Yet this was exactly the kind of relationship Callie had sought in the months since her divorce. But suddenly, hearing Jared lay out that kind of temporary affair in black-and-white terms—

Made the opposite sound, well, nice, even as the thought of anything more permanent than a piece of tape scared the heck out of her. But when she looked at Jared—nice, safe, sweet Jared—she wondered if maybe it were possible that she'd been overlooking a good guy all along.

"I wonder if we're both lying to ourselves, Jared. In a way."

His eyes widened in surprise. "Lying?"

"My friends have this crazy idea that I should be looking for Mr. Right." She let out a little laugh. "They even made a bet with me that I'd find him."

Jared didn't say anything for a long moment. Then he coughed and shook his head. "Did you just say Mr. Right? As in the guy you're going to marry, buy a house with, then have kids and get a Labrador with, Mr. Right?"

She nodded. "It's sort of, ah, a dare. I told you, the whole thing was insane."

"A dare?"

"The other women who work at the Wedding Belles, all believe Mr. Right exists. After all, it's practically part of the job description. And they challenged me to find him. Because…" Her voice trailed off. Why tell him all this? What woman poured out her whole sad can't find the right man story?

"Go ahead, tell me more."

Jared, though, seemed genuinely interested. And he hadn't gone running down the nearest highway or faked his own death, both good signs of a noncommitment phobic man. Maybe he was indulging her or maybe he truly wanted to hear what she had to say.

"Because I'm a little jaded, to say the least, and because I'm the least settled out of all of us. I've met my fair share of Mr. Wrongs. One in particular."

"I know." Sympathy flooded his words, another beacon of their shared history. Callie wondered how wise it was to connect with a man who knew her past, who knew about all her mistakes.

They'd reached the restaurant and the conversation paused while Jared opened the door for her. There was a brief wait, then the maître d' led them to a table.

"And if you find this Mr. Right," Jared said after they were seated and had their drinks, "are you going to marry him?"

Callie nearly choked on the sip of soda in her mouth. "I, ah, hadn't thought that far. And no, that really wasn't in my plans, not again. I already took that road and it led nowhere. You know me, Jared. I'm not a mortgage-signing, minivan-buying kind of person."

Jared grinned. "Don't tell me you'd let your Mr. Perfect get away, and send that one ideal fish back into the dating waters?"

The thought of marrying again, of making that

commitment—and possibly being wrong and ending up heartbroken all over again—still terrified her. Add that into the thought of staying in one place, committed to another man—

Callie shook her head. "I'll, ah, cross that bridge when I get to it."

"So your goal is to test the waters, more or less. See if there is such a thing as a right person for everyone?"

"Yes."

He laced his fingers together, then laid his hands on the table. "What if I could prove to you that true love existed?"

"Prove it to me? How?"

"I'm a man of science. You're a woman who takes very little on faith, at least where relationships are concerned. I'd like to show you, beyond a reasonable doubt, that true love does, in fact, exist."

"Like Santa Claus, UFOs and Big Foot?"

"Well, those might be a bit beyond even my capabilities." He took a sip of his soda, then continued. "But I do think it is possible to quantify love. Don't you?"

"As in measure it, weigh it, show it in a tangible manner?" Callie shook her head. "No, sorry, I don't."

Jared leaned closer, and though they were separated by a table in a public restaurant, the intimacy between them increased a dozen degrees. "Then let me prove it to you."

"Prove it to me?" She shook her head. "I've heard those words before, Jared. And I got proof of the exact opposite."

He reached out and touched her hand. Nothing in that connection spoke of charts and data, as far as Callie was concerned. What did Jared want? And for that matter, what did she want? "I'm not Tony, Callie."

She glanced away, thinking of the terrible way her marriage had ended, the bright hopes that had been dashed so quickly, the illusions that had been shattered nearly as quickly as the ring had been slipped on her finger. "No, you're not."

"And we had a wonderful time the other night, didn't we?"

She nodded.

"That one night in college, we had chemistry between us, right?"

Chemistry, biology, physics and the entire range of earth sciences. Oh, yeah. Callie nodded again.

"And since then we've both gotten older," Jared said, his voice deepening. "And more experienced."

Heat infused Callie's body. She knew exactly what he meant…and exactly where he could apply that experience, given half the chance. "Where are you going with this?"

"Then why are you so scared to be with me? Haven't I always been a good friend?"

"Yeah," she said, disappointment once again hitting her square in the chest. A friend, he was only a friend. That should, indeed, be all that she wanted. It kept her on the safe relationship ground she liked, kept her heart from being risked, kept her from getting emotionally involved. "You've always been a good friend."

He nodded, as if that were the answer he'd expected. Jared paused for a moment, then returned his attention to her. "I'm glad you're doing this. Looking for Mr. Right. You deserve a good man. Tony was…" He shook his head. "Let's just say I didn't foresee a happy ending whenever he dated someone."

"What do you mean?"

"Tony had a problem with monogamy. Always did."

The words stung, even though Callie should have been used to them by now. Her divorce had happened over a year in the past, the marriage over long before the piece of paper made it legally so. Her ex-husband's betrayals were common knowledge to her by now, but somehow, coming from Jared, someone who knew her from before, it seemed to hurt all over again. "Why didn't you ever say anything?"

"Would you have believed me?"

She thought of how infatuated she had been with Tony. How he'd seemed to represent everything she wanted. The very symbol of escape from the life she hated. She'd seen him as a savior, a hero—when he'd been anything but. She sighed. "No."

"I tried, a hundred times, to say something, but…" He drew in a breath. "I couldn't break your heart."

Somehow, that touched her in a way she hadn't expected. She thought of the Jared she'd known then, a shyer, quieter man, less sure of himself, someone who kept to himself yet was true to those he made his friends. "Maybe it would have been better if you had."

"It probably would have. And I was wrong. I'm sorry, Callie."

"It's okay." She smiled. "My mother always said I was the kind of hardheaded kid who had to learn the stove was hot by burning my own hand."

He chuckled. "And I was the kind who nearly blew it up trying to test the boiling points of different liquids."

She cocked her head, studying him. "We're very different people, aren't we, Jared?"

His gaze met hers, deep blue eyes so vibrant, for

a moment she felt as if she could swim in the ocean of his gaze. "Not so different, not always. I used to wish, though, that you noticed me more. Back in those days. Realized I was more than just your lab partner in high school. Once we turned off the Bunsen burner, you pretty much forgot I existed." He shrugged, as if it didn't matter, but Callie could tell it had. "That's okay. I was…not exactly stud of the year back then."

Had she done that? She remembered being, as he'd said, lab partners with Jared, working on science projects, conducting experiments, filling out worksheets. Other than that, they'd gone their separate ways in high school, she with her friends, then with Tony. Then, later, in college, he'd been in different classes altogether, except for the one class they'd been stuck in together—Humanities and Modern Thinking, where they'd both struggled under a difficult professor and sought each other's help once again, resurrecting the old friendship—

And a new, stronger connection.

Until Tony had come back and Callie had fallen into her old patterns, leaving Jared behind.

She reached for him across the table, knowing nine years had passed and a few words couldn't make up for what had happened back then. "I'm sorry, too, Jared."

"It was nothing. I grew up to be a reasonably well-adjusted adult." He grinned, but once again she got the feeling that she had hurt him in those years and remorse settled heavy on her shoulders. "What you said earlier, about wondering whether there was such a thing as one right person for everyone, is sort of the theory I'm working on."

"Your theory?"

He nodded. "That's what I was doing in the bar. I'm a researcher for Wiley Games, and this time, I was researching love—in a way."

Callie nearly spit onto Jared. "You? Researching love?"

"Hey, it's not that unbelievable." He cleared his throat and something unreadable washed over his gaze. "Not love *exactly,* more love games. The way couples get to know each other. Wiley is using my data to create a bedroom game. I see that face. Don't laugh."

But she did anyway.

"I'm hoping to use some of the research for serious purposes, too. Down the road I hope to extrapolate enough information from the data to write a research paper." He shrugged. "Give some credentials to the whole thing. Something that goes beyond 'Twenty Tantalizing Bedroom Teasers.'"

"That's what you were doing when I ran into you?"

He nodded. "I've already interviewed several dozen couples. The trouble is finding people who are happy together."

"I know plenty of those," Callie said. "We have a database of past clients at Wedding Belles and if there's one thing they love to talk about, it's how they met and got to know each other. If you want, I can put you in touch with some of them."

"I'd appreciate that. It'll expedite my research. It'll be just like the old days," Jared said. "You and me, study partners again. In a way."

"If I remember right, I wasn't much help when it came to studying for those Humanities tests. It was like the blind leading the blind. Don't you think that might not be the best idea?"

"It won't be anything but friends working together, just like the old days."

"Friends who go on dates."

He pushed his glasses up on his nose, as if the mention of that disconcerted him.

"And doesn't that take us out of the realm of friends?"

Jared's cool returned and he met her gaze head-on. "Does it?"

Callie wasn't quite sure herself where she and Jared were right now. All she knew was that a confusing jumble of feelings rushed through her every time he touched her, looked at her. Those were just as quickly chased by the reminder that Jared had been a good friend for years, and this could be a temporary rush of hormones and nothing more. They were very different people, who wanted very different things, which meant they could never be a couple.

Right?

"Have you decided what you'd like to order?" The waiter's voice cut through the tension between Callie and Jared, drawing them back to mundane items.

"Uh…" Callie glanced down at the menu, realizing she hadn't even opened it yet.

Jared gave her a smile. "Lasagna, extra sauce on the side?"

Once again, he'd read her mind. If the man sent out any more confusing signals, he'd be a blindfolded air traffic controller. "Yes."

After the waiter was gone, Callie turned back to Jared. "So, will you help me?"

She considered him. What could it hurt, really? Spending time with Jared would get her friends off her back about that silly bet and if it didn't work out, would give her the ammunition she needed to once again prove that there was no such thing as true love for everyone. And if it did…well, she'd cross that bridge when she got to it, as she'd said earlier. "Okay. I'll help you, but only for a week. This is the busy season for weddings."

"It's okay. Any help is great."

"Is that enough time, though?"

He grinned. "I don't see why not. Most all the couples I interviewed said that's how it always happened for them. They met, and within the first few minutes of conversation, they just…knew."

Like with a kiss?

If Jared had kissed her the other night, would she have known something then, just as she had felt a connection all those years ago on that one night they'd spent together?

Had it been that special link he was talking about or simply a hormonal overload?

Jared put out his hand. "Let's shake on it."

She took his and did as he asked. It should have been just a simple touch, a sealing of a deal, but when his palm touched hers, Callie's pulse ratcheted up again. "This has to be the weirdest start to a relationship I've ever seen."

"Although, this is more of a partnership, isn't it?" Jared's gaze met hers. "That way, we're clear from the start, and no one gets hurt."

Something flickered in his eyes, and Callie knew—knew for sure now—that she *had* hurt him all those years ago.

Had she read leftover feelings in his touch? Had

he never really forgotten her? Never gotten over her?

And if so, where did that leave them?

The waiter brought their lasagna. Steam rose in curls off the pasta, bringing with it the tangy scent of tomato sauce and the sharp notes of parmesan cheese. Callie's stomach rumbled in anticipation.

After they'd each had a few bites, Jared returned his attention to Callie. Every time he did that, it was as if a giant spotlight had shone on her. "So what did you do before you became a florist?"

"Everything. I flopped at burger flipping. Had a problem with authority figures telling me how to apply ketchup."

Jared laughed. "Seriously?"

"I wasn't cut out for fast food. Or grocery packing. Or a number of other jobs. In fact, my personal résumé is pretty cluttered with holes and temporary employment. Thank goodness I found a field I love and a boss I love working for." Callie buttered a piece of bread, then gestured toward Jared. "What about you? I take it you never veered from the Mr. Straight-and-Narrow path?"

"And why would you guess that?"

"Because I know you, Jared. And because everything about you has always screamed Straight-and-Narrow. The suit, the glasses, the clipboard in a bar, for Pete's sake."

"What's wrong with a suit?"

"Nothing. Nothing at all." In fact, he made a suit look good. Really, really good.

"I admit, I followed the regular route. College, then straight into suit-and-tie world."

"How far did you go in college?"

His gaze met hers. "After I left UMass, I went to CalState, then on to Stanford, and got my master's, then my PhD. On scholarships, thankfully, because I never could have paid my own way. There's an advantage to having good grades."

"I wish I'd finished."

"You dropped out?"

"I've never been one for staying in one place for long and once Tony and I eloped, we were off and running all over the world." She took a bite of food. "This job here is the longest I've been anywhere."

"Why?"

"You know me, Jared. Five minutes in a room and I go stir-crazy." It had been part of what had attracted her to Tony. His constant wanderlust, quest for something new every day. But when she'd divorced him, Callie had made the decision to settle down, plant some roots, at least for a while. So far, she hadn't done anything more permanent than sign a month-to-month lease on her apartment.

"You should have gotten your degree," Jared said. "You were really smart. You did great in Science."

"Thanks to you."

"No, it wasn't me. You had all the brains you needed, Callie."

She looked away, fiddled with her bread. "You were the only reason I ever passed the Periodic Table of Elements test."

"You were the one who made studying for it fun. Who else could turn that into a game?"

"It was pretty boring stuff, you have to admit."

"Okay, it was. But you made it fun." His gaze connected with hers again. "And that's what I want more of."

"More Science? You didn't get enough of E equals mc squared?"

"No. More of the fun you. The wild and crazy Callie I remembered from high school. When we were together…" He paused, drew in a breath, and in the space of that moment, Callie knew something was coming, something she didn't want to hear. "You brought out a side of me that, well, that I wasn't even aware existed."

"What do you mean?"

"I was your resident geek. You were the wild child. All these years, I've stayed the same. So while we're working together, maybe a little of that wildness could rub off like it did the other night—"

"That night was a once in a lifetime thing," Callie said, putting up her hand. "I'm not planning on repeating that."

"Why not?"

"I've changed, Jared. I'm not who I used to be." How could she tell him that doing that had awakened a part of her she'd worked very hard to keep quiet? That she was afraid of becoming the woman who ran out on people at a moment's notice, the one who couldn't stay put? She had friends here, a job—but that itch to leave, to move on, had never really left her.

"No one changes that much."

That scared her, and tempted her, and exactly why Callie didn't want to go poking around in her past, even with Mr. Straight-and-Narrow Jared.

"I did. So if you're looking for that Callie," she said, her gaze connecting with his, leaving no room for misinterpretation, "she doesn't exist anymore."

"Maybe she should," Jared said. "Because I miss her. Very much."

And in those words, he issued Callie a challenge that half of her very much wanted to take.

CHAPTER SIX

JARED rubbed at his eyes, then leaned back in his chair so far, the office seat tipped precariously on its wheels and let out a creak of warning. The numbers before him swam in a jumble, the words on the screen a blur, but the workload had yet to reduce.

"Dude, you have zero life. You're like one of those Byzantine bald guys."

Jared turned. "Byzantine bald guys?"

Pope, Jared's college intern, spun around a second chair and draped his lean stonewashed jean-clad legs over either side. "Yeah, you know those guys who wear those funny robes and go around chanting all the time."

"You mean monks?" Jared shook his head. "I don't think my love life is that bad."

"Last time you had a date, man had taken his first steps on the moon."

Jared made a face at the spiky-haired blonde. "I'm not even that old."

Pope looked surprised. "Really? 'Cuz, dude, I thought you were at least, like, fifty."

"Thirty-three, Pope. The moon walk was in sixty-nine."

Pope flipped out his fingers, did a little counting. Jared bit back a groan at hiring the intern. The kid had zero common sense, almost no personal skills, but was a whiz with computer programs. If only his technological prowess extended into other areas of his brain. "My bad. Guess you weren't around then. Still, you are like total hermit guy. You need a chick."

"Women aren't chicks, Pope."

Pope shrugged. "Whatever. They aren't PCs either and that's about the only thing you've been intimate with since I started working here." Pope put up his hands. "Now if that's your thing, dude, I'm all for free expression—"

"No!"

"It's cool, it's cool. Totally. You struck me as the straight and narrow type anyway."

"Straight and narrow," Jared repeated. The same thing Callie had said at lunch today. He sighed. "Yeah, that's me."

Except for those few songs on the stage the other night, he was as straight as a fence post. The only time he'd done anything wild had been in college, and all he'd done then was put on a leather jacket, sit astride a Harley and pretend to be a biker for Halloween. He'd ended up on a stage with her, then spending one incredible, amazing night with Callie, only to have her leave for another man in the morning.

And look where that one night of daredevil living had gotten him.

He glanced at the computer beside him. In an intimate relationship with a nineteen-inch monitor.

"Yo, dude, you ever need help with the ladies, call me. I'm a regular Lethargio."

Jared spun back toward Pope. "Don't you mean Lothario?"

"Hell, no. Lethargio. I lay back, and the ladies just come to me." Pope spread his arms wide. "I got the goods, dude. The look, the car, the personality. You on the other hand, could use a little help in those areas."

"What's wrong with the way I look? My car?" Jared wasn't about to compare personalities. He was quite happy with his.

Pope pitched forward and flicked at the tie around Jared's neck. "For one, the strangled chicken look does not scream sexy. For another, pleated pants are advertisements for balloons."

Jared glanced down at his striped tie, his pleated khakis. When he'd gotten dressed this morning, the choices had seemed…normal. The kind of thing he wore every day.

Maybe that was the problem. The clothes he pulled out of his closet were the ones he pulled out every day, had chosen for years on end. He shopped in the same department of the same store, year after year. No deviation from the regular pattern.

He glanced over at Pope. The intern's button-down shirt was open at the neck, untucked, but managed to have a wilder, more approachable look. His jeans were not too tight, but snug enough that a woman looking at Pope would know the guy worked out. No balloon advertisements there.

"Where do you shop?" Jared asked.

"Abercrombie. Hollister. Some Hot Topic, though I'm more a Banana Republic kind of guy when I'm in the flush with the dough."

Jared stared at Pope. Those were names of stores? They had to be on a whole other level of the mall. Maybe in an entirely different mall than the one Jared went to. "Uh, where would I find Abercrumb?"

Pope laughed and popped out of his chair. "Dude, you may be the professor in here, but when it comes to scoring with chicks, you are a total Gilligan."

On Sunday afternoon Callie and Julie rode back from the spacious Markson home in Newton, the

Wedding Belles van empty of flowers, but still carrying the scent of the dozens of arrangements and bouquets. "I can't believe we pulled that one off," Callie said. "Another amazing Belles wedding."

Julie shifted in her seat to face Callie and grinned. "Every one of them is amazing, aren't they?"

Callie nodded, then flipped on her directional to turn right onto Boylston Street and head back toward the shop. "When I first started working for Belle, I was astounded at how she could pull something out of nothing. A bride and groom come into the Wedding Belles shop with a simple idea—"

"Sometimes not even that."

"And then Belle and the rest of us took that idea and made it into something like what we just saw."

Julie sighed. "Something magical." She leaned back against the seat, then removed the clip atop her head, releasing her long, curly chestnut hair from its prison. It tumbled past her shoulders. Julie always complained about her locks, but Callie thought her hair was beautiful. "It makes you believe, doesn't it?"

Callie stopped for a red light. "Believe in what?"

"Happy endings. Riding off into the sunset."

"Julie, you get like this after every one of our weddings. All misty-eyed."

Julie turned to her. "And you don't?"

Callie shrugged. "I'm more of a realist." The light changed and Callie moved forward—-inched forward, really, with the rest of the slow-moving traffic, turning onto Fairfield. No matter the time of day, downtown Boston always seemed to move at a snail's pace.

"You must have believed at some point. You got married, too."

"I eloped. There's a difference."

"What difference?"

"A stupid mistake difference. A one-night, thinking-he-was-the-one, difference." Rain started to fall, so Callie flipped on the wipers and rolled up her window. She thought of the wedding the Belles were all planning on throwing for Julie, the secret so good, she nearly burst with wanting to tell it, but knew that keeping it would make it all so much more fun when Julie's wedding day came and she saw the fabulous day planned by her friends.

"And then what happened?" Julie said, drawing Callie's attention back to Callie's love life.

"Can we just drop it? My ex is not exactly my favorite topic of conversation." Callie let out a sigh, then turned to Julie. "Sorry. I'm just not in the best of moods. I've got a lot on my mind."

"Your mom again?"

Callie's shoulders sagged, and tears rushed to the back of her eyes. Leave it to her friend to guess, to get right to the heart of the matter. "Yeah. How'd you know?"

"I know you, Cal. That's all it takes."

"She's divorcing husband number four and flying into town to see me in a few days. She needs a shoulder to cry on. Again."

"Number four?"

"My mother really likes weddings, too." Callie tried to work up a smile, but it fell flat. She made the turn onto Newbury Street, and started looking for street-side parking in front of the shop, not an easy thing to find on a rainy day. "She just picks a lot of Mr. Wrongs."

"Well, no wonder." Julie's voice had softened.

"No wonder what?"

"No wonder you're so afraid of doing the same thing again."

"I'm not afraid." Callie drew in a breath, let it out. "Okay, I am. The other night I went over to O'Malley's to deliver the invitations for his daughter's wedding and ran into a guy I used to know. Then, at the poker game the other night, Audra and the other girls made me agree to date him, after I had the losing hand."

Julie laughed. "Never bet against Audra. But how did you know this guy?"

"We were friends, and we went out on one date, years and years ago."

"And how is Mr. Past now?"

"Nice. He was always…nice."

"And that, I take it, was the problem? He was nice, but not…exciting?"

"He has his exciting…moments," Callie said, thinking of that night in college. A totally exciting moment, with a Jared so unlike the one she'd thought she'd known.

"So what are you going to do?"

"Well, I wasn't going to do anything, but then…" She parked the van in front of the Wedding Belles office and shut off the engine. "He came to me with a proposition."

"A proposition? As in 'hey baby, come up and see my etchings' kind of proposition?"

Callie laughed. "No. He's a research scientist and he wants me to help him find couples that he can interview. He's asking them questions about how they met, and what made them stay together."

"Ooh, how romantic." Julie made a face. "Not."

"Well, after Jared left, I got to thinking." She smiled, and the wheels in Callie's head began to turn. For the first time in a long time, she was intrigued. Jared's question had made her wonder about what she had put aside over the past three years. Had she simply been sitting still?

Could it be possible to light that fire in herself—a fire that seemed to have been extinguished by her divorce—without it erupting into the full-force flames of running for the hills? Could she maybe dip into who she used to be, find a bit of that magic she had lost when Tony broke her heart, without losing her newfound life? And in the meantime, maybe make things up to Jared a little?

"What if I took the professor's proposition and messed with his research?"

"How are you intending to do that?"

"What if I turn the tables on him? Maybe take him beyond a little data on hand holding and kissing?"

Julie nodded, putting the pieces together. "And make *his* blood pressure ratchet up?"

"Exactly. In other words, this lab rat puts the *professor* into the maze, at least a little. Jared says he misses the wild side of me and that he wants a little more fun in his life." Callie grinned. "If that's the case, then I have a few experiments of my own I want to conduct. And they'll be fun, but *my* kind of fun."

"You're sure about this?" Jared said. He sent the contraption a dubious glance.

"Absolutely." Callie handed the attendant six tickets, then grasped Jared's hand and got in line behind the dozen children. "Are you *brave* enough for this?"

He tossed her a grin. "Are *you?*"

"Baby, I was born brave."

When she looked at him like that, Jared's gut tightened and he thought of kissing her again. Not just once, but a hundred times. And taking her everywhere but to an amusement park.

Totally not part of the plan. He was supposed to be here to work on his research, to use that to keep his distance, so he could keep his heart out of the fray again. He was a smart man—and a smart man knew enough not to make the same mistake twice.

Just then, the gate opened, the children surged forward and Callie led him onto the platform. They slipped inside a giant curved seat, the sign above it reading Tilt-A-Whirl in a rainbow of letters.

"Grab the center wheel," she told him, "and hold on to your lunch."

He glanced around at their metal surroundings. "Do you know the last time they did a maintenance check? Tightened the bolts? Lubricated the fittings?"

"Quit worrying and just enjoy the ride. Besides, they have him to worry about that." Callie gestured toward the ride attendant, who loped across the platform, checking each of the seats.

Jared cast a doubtful look at the grease-stained, tattered-shirt youth shuffling through his job. "When was the last time he had a drug test?"

Callie laughed. "Has anyone told you that you worry too much?"

"Statistically—"

Callie pressed a finger to Jared's lips. "Focus on having fun, Jared. Not on statistics."

"I'm focused," he said. "But not on the ride." He reached up one hand—the ride, the noisy park, the warm spring evening—all of it forgotten in the space of the second her touch had met his lips, when the car they were in jerked to a start, thrusting Callie against his chest.

"Hold on tight," she whispered.

His arm came down and wrapped around her. "Exactly what I was thinking."

Jared quickly found it harder to do that than he'd expected. The Tilt-A-Whirl began to pick up tempo, matching the rock music pounding out of the sound system. Centrifugal force whipped them around the circle, then Callie reached forward and grabbed the wheel, one hand reaching over the other, spinning it faster and faster, in turn spinning their seat, increasing their circles.

The force flattened her to his chest, but the thrill made her laugh. Jared stopped worrying about bolts and safety inspections and found himself caught in Callie's infectious spirit, his hands walking over hers, increasing the spin factor.

"Having fun?" she called over the music.

"Absolutely."

"Let's go faster then." And she grabbed faster, the dare in her green eyes encouraging him to do the same.

He matched her speed, joining her in laughter, their car whipping in a wild spiral that matched the growing desire in Jared's veins. He glanced over at her, wanting Callie in a way he couldn't remember ever wanting her before.

This wasn't the heated intensity of a college crush. It wasn't the what-if thoughts of a man who had lost a woman to someone else. It wasn't the instant connection of meeting up with a long-lost love. This was full-on, holy-cow, get-off-this-ride and go-somewhere-alone lust.

And then, the music began to ebb, the ride began to slow, the car's spin going from high-speed wash cycle to low-gear and then finally stop. The attendant climbed back onto the platform, but the children had already gotten out of their seats and clambered past him, dashing back to their parents, exclaiming about how much fun they'd had. One little boy stumbled down the steps, clutching his stomach and moaning about too much cotton candy.

Callie turned to Jared, laughter dancing in her eyes. "That was fun."

"It was." A heartbeat passed between them. He knew they should get out of there. Make room for the next flock of kids. But he wasn't ready to leave, not yet.

"Do you want to tackle the Ferris wheel or the—" She stared at him, their little world cocooned in the semiprivate wall of ride. "What? Do I have some mustard on my lips or something?"

"Or something." Jared leaned forward and before he could think about what he was doing, kissed Callie.

When Jared kissed Callie, the world shuddered to a stop. All the thoughts and emotions that had been swirling in her mind, the war of should-she or shouldn't-she screeching to a halt, with one big neon, oh-yes-she-should.

Jared's mouth drifted over hers, at first light and easy, as soft as a cloud, then, when she opened more against him, he gathered her into his arms, pressing her to his chest.

His kiss deepened and she inhaled his warm, male scent, memory spiraling her back all those years, to every one of their touches, as if they'd never been apart, as if she'd never chosen another. She reached up, her hands tangling in his hair, fire rushing through her veins, igniting parts of her that had felt dead for so long, so very, very long.

He cupped her jaw, a tender, sweet gesture that nearly made Callie cry, and then drifted his lips over hers, before coming back to kiss her again, thoroughly, tenderly.

Like a woman should be kissed. Like a man who took his time. Who cared that the woman enjoyed the kiss.

And everything within Callie sang better than her voice had sounded on that stage.

For Jared, kissing Callie rocked him to the core. The analytical part of his mind told himself to measure this kiss. Her response. His own increased heartbeat, rapid pulse. Make it part of his research, stay uninvolved.

The other half of him told the analytical part to shut the hell up for at least five seconds.

And he did, enjoying the feel of her in his arms, the way she curved into his body, the way everything about Callie had always fit exactly right. Fire raced through his veins, ignited every part of his brain, his heart. And told him he was no longer looking at her with the eyes of a researcher.

Jared drew back, his heart thudding hard.

Callie smiled at him. "So, was that part of the grand experiment? Or part of the ride?"

"Oh, you're not part of the experiment at all."

He lied.

He had made Callie part of the research. And he needed to keep it that way. Only by putting his research between them, the familiar world of numbers, could he erect a wall strong enough to protect his heart. Then maybe he wouldn't fall as hard for her as he had before.

Nothing killed a libido faster than a spreadsheet, after all. So, a little note-taking, some analysis of some figures—and hopefully he'd forget all about how sexy her figure was.

It was the only option. After all, Jared knew he hadn't turned into the kind of man Callie wanted. He was, as always, Mr. Straight-and-Narrow.

Unfortunately Mr. Straight-and-Narrow still had a major thing for Ms. Wild-and-Crazy.

He couldn't seem to stop wanting to see her, to keep asking her out. The only solution was to make her part of the numbers, to keep his focus on work. Not an impossible situation, but one where he already knew the probable relationship outcome if he didn't stick to his research guns.

Failure.

"Oh, look, Jared. There's a bunch of couples over there. Maybe you should go talk to them?"

"Oh, yeah," Jared said, trying to draw himself back to work, and away from how amazing Callie looked in jeans and a V-necked T-shirt. He fumbled for his notepad, his pen. Where had his pen gone? It must have slipped out when the ride was flinging them against each other. "I seem to have lost my pen."

"Right here," Callie said, leaning past him, her breasts brushing against his chest, and sending his thoughts way past research territory and down a whole other path that had nothing to do with science and a whole lot to do with anatomy. "You were, ah, sitting on it." Her voice had gone husky, throaty. If he didn't know better, he'd swear she was flirting with him.

"Oh, yeah. Uh, thanks."

She placed it in his palm, her eyes a tease. "No problem. Just doing my job as a research assistant."

"Mister, are you going to get out of there or what?"

They turned and saw a chubby ten-year-old boy standing outside their car, his arms crossed over his chest.

Jared shoved his glasses up on his nose. "We should probably go."

"Unless you want to ride again?" Callie offered.

Everything within him did. But he'd already run this test once. There was no scientific reason to do it again. "No, I'm good."

"As long as you're sure." Then she slipped out of the car and—

Jared was sure, she sauntered off the platform and away from him.

Callie *was* flirting with him?

Was she truly interested in him? He was the one who had started this game, opened this particular can of worms. And now, he didn't know which way it was going. Every time he tried to read her, he seemed to get a different story. He'd gone into this with one hypothesis. That love could be manufactured, measured. That he could stay detached, out of the fray of the experiment.

But with every sway of Callie's hips, Jared knew he was wrong. He was feeling about as detached as a fly caught in a spider's web.

"Let's get something to eat," Callie said, taking Jared's hand and leading him toward a stand-alone hut labeled Snack Shack. The scent of deep fried foods wafted off the small building, with people crowded around it, shouting out orders for things called "elephant ears."

Lord help him. Fried elephant parts?

"I am not getting an elephant ear," Jared said, his stomach rolling at the thought.

Callie laughed. "You haven't lived until you've had one."

"Are you crazy?"

"Trust me." Her green eyes met his, and his objections melted away. She turned back toward the

Snack Shack, put up two fingers, had her money out and had paid for two of the treats before Jared could stop her. When the lady behind the trailer window handed them over, Callie spooned on some canned cinnamon apples, then sprinkled the tops with confectionary sugar and gave one to Jared. "Your elephant ear."

He looked down at the bubbled fried disc on the plate. Not gray, but tan, thank God, like bread. "I take it this isn't real fried ear?"

Callie laughed. "No. It's a glob of fried dough. Really bad for your arteries and your heart."

As Jared watched Callie's generous crimson mouth close around a bite of the treat and felt desire stir anew, he knew the fried dough wasn't the only thing bad for his heart.

He kept losing track of his reason for being with her. He'd gone into this project with every intention of keeping his emotions separate. He'd thought, because he'd been down this road with Callie before, that he could compartmentalize his heart from the data. Remind himself not to fall in love again.

Uh-huh. And how well was that plan working?

"Doesn't it tempt you?"

Callie's voice drew Jared back to the present. "Tempt me?" Oh, he was tempted all right. That was the problem.

"Yeah, the elephant ear. They're best when they're hot."

"Oh, yes. Well, you know me. Knife and fork guy all the way." He gave her a grin.

"I thought you wanted to loosen up." Callie leaned forward and flipped his tie. "That means in all aspects. You did it once, remember?"

Jared stepped away, reaching for a set of plastic silverware and a napkin. He gestured toward a picnic table and they each took a seat. "That was a long time ago and it was only for one night."

"Then what was that back in the karaoke bar?"

He grinned. "An aberration."

"The professor loosening his tie after a couple of beers?"

"Something like that." If he was smart, he'd remember to keep his tie tight, and his glasses on. That one foray into the leather jacket had been a mistake. He'd tried to become the kind of guy he'd thought Callie would want—

And she'd left him for a real heartbreaker instead.

He knew better. Knew where walking on the wild side got a man. Why had he ever told her he wanted to add a little wildness to his life? The minute he'd done that—

He'd kissed her.

Jared led a cautious, predictable life for a reason.

Get back to the research. The reason for being here, he reminded himself. Which meant getting close to her, touching her. But not kissing her. Keeping it impersonal.

All in the name of data, of course.

They'd finished their snacks and tossed away the paper plates. Jared stood and slipped his hand into Callie's, the warm feeling of her palm against his sending his mind off track again. "What next?"

A devilish gleam lit her eyes. "Whatever scares you most."

"That's easy." He caught her gaze. "You."

"Me?"

The crowd parted around them, like waves breaking past rocks, the neon lights of the amusement park flashed their rainbow dance across Callie's features, while the rock music of the rides played a rhythmic undertow in the background.

"Why do I scare you?"

"For one," he said, taking a step closer, picking up her other hand, pulling her to the side, out of the fray, "you can sing my pants off. For another, you can tilt that Tilt-A-Whirl like nobody's business."

Beneath his grasp, her pulse ratcheted up, her breathing quickened. Jared made mental notes, but they kept getting jumbled, and he wondered how clear his data would be later. And whether he even cared.

"I had a good partner in crime," Callie said. "Shall we try another ride?"

Jared should say no. He had mountains of work ahead of him tonight. The normal Jared begged off early from a date, went back to his apartment, holed up at his little desk with his laptop and a cold sandwich and worked until the wee hours of the morning. For years, he'd found his job relatively satisfying and rewarding. Loved the challenge of numbers and data.

But for some reason, being with Callie again had awakened an old itch for something crazy, a dangerous feeling, the one that had once made him consider ditching his ambitions and forgetting every shred of responsibility.

Surely, though, he could do that for a few hours. What would it hurt? He could make up the hours tomorrow. The next day.

But what he couldn't make up was this moment, the way Callie looked right this second.

"The Ferris wheel," he said. "I've never been on one."

"Never? Really? Who goes through life missing out on the Ferris wheel?"

"Me, I guess." He didn't elaborate. A guy didn't need to open the book of his childhood to know it wasn't the kind of story other people wanted to read.

"Well then," Callie said. "Let me show you what you've been missing out on." She led him through the crowds and down the popcorn-strewn path toward the flashing Ferris wheel. It reached three stories up into the air, spinning in a slow, lazy circle, the carts swinging back and forth, filled with necking teenagers, families and elderly couples. "Think you're man enough for this one?"

"Oh, I think I can handle it. If you can."

"Absolutely." She handed their tickets to the ticket taker, who looked like he could have been an older, more tired carbon copy of the one who'd worked the Tilt-A-Whirl. The man reached out, stopped one of the metal seats, then waited while Callie and Jared climbed inside. The bar lowered over their laps, then the ride began its slow backward journey. In a few seconds, the amusement park had disappeared, the people, rides, games of chance shrinking with each upward movement of the wheel.

Soon they were at the top. The car stopped, swaying slightly as the cool spring breeze whistled through the car. "It's chilly up this high," Callie said.

"Here." Jared drew her against him. She fit perfectly, as he'd known she would. Just like she used to. "Is that better?"

"Yes." Callie tipped her chin to face him. "Thank you."

"My pleasure." The stars above reflected in her

eyes, the moon danced on her features. Jared's research seemed a thousand miles away.

"Have those couples worked out? The names I gave you?" Callie asked.

It took Jared a second to make the connection with what she was talking about. "Couples?"

"For the game. Your research, remember?"

Oh, he was researching, all right. Every single thing *Callie* was doing. Then he remembered. Callie had given him several names earlier that day. Jared had already completed two interviews. "They were great contacts. Thank you."

"Good." She beamed. "I'm glad to help. If you're looking for any other specific couple types, I can—"

"I don't want to talk about research right now." He pulled her closer.

"Oh." She let out a slight gasp, her mouth opening in surprise, then a smile. "Oh, okay."

The temptation between them ratcheted up a thousand times. To hell with the plan. With staying out of the experiment. With staying neutral, uninvolved. Jared lowered his head, brushed his lips against hers, intending only to kiss her sweetly, softly, but just as quickly realizing he was definitely unable to stop there.

Because he knew how good it would be. Knew what it was like to kiss Callie. To taste her.

And before his better judgment could take the lead, he opened his mouth against hers, his other hand coming up to cup her jaw, his thumb sliding along the delicate edge.

She arched slightly against him, and fire exploded in Jared's brain. For a man who lived his life on strictly analytical terms, it was a heady rush, a journey into a new land, one he'd forgotten existed.

But the very one that had led to him making some very foolish mistakes.

Jared pulled back, just as the ride began to move again with a shudder. He pushed his glasses up on his nose, and straightened his tie, the actions making him feel like himself again.

At least the outside was orderly.

"Sorry," he said. "I didn't mean to lose control, to take things further than—"

"You and your control." Callie shook her head, clearly frustrated with him. "You keep telling me you want to be a little wilder, to loosen up, and yet every time you're with me, you're all research and Mr. Professor again. What's it going to take to get you to let up, Jared? To go back to the guy you were that one night in college?"

"Maybe that was a mistake. An early midlife crisis or something." He thought of how it had ended, of how she'd woken up the next morning and told him what a mistake they had made.

How foolish he had felt, looking at that leather jacket lying over the chair in the bedroom, a silly, empty shell. In the light of day, revealed for what it was—just a costume. Realizing he'd tried to be someone he wasn't. Only to lose Callie in the end anyway.

"What if that was the *real* you? And this—" she tugged on his tie "—isn't?"

"Are we talking about getting real? Because I seem to remember a different Callie from those days myself. You used to be completely spontaneous. Run off to a party at the drop of a hat. Would take a weekend in Vegas, a trip to the beach, just about anything, just because someone asked you to. What happened to that Callie?"

She looked away, avoiding his gaze, the subject at hand. He'd hit a nerve, clearly. "I went to the bar and sang Madonna with you. That's spontaneous."

"So is buying name brand detergent without a coupon." Their seat swung toward the front of the Ferris wheel, then stopped to let off some people at the bottom. Jared wondered why he was pushing Callie on this topic so much.

Why did he care if she had changed? Why was he pushing so hard to have back the old Callie?

The very woman who had walked out on him and married his best friend?

Because he was one serious glutton for punishment, that was clear. So he cleared his throat and returned again to the world he knew, the safe territory of statistics and numbers. "On the other hand, my studies have shown a little spontaneity can be good for a relation—"

"Stop," Callie said, as their ride started and stopped, bringing them closer and closer to the debarking point. "Tell me one thing, Jared. What does spontaneity have to do with your research project?"

"It has everything to do with it. Falling in love is a spontaneous act."

"Oh, yeah?" She arched a brow. Their car had swung into place and the attendant stepped forward to raise the bar, releasing them from the seat. "And tell me exactly how you know this. Because you read it in some scholarly journal or because you have actually done it yourself? Because I *have* fallen in love at first sight. And it was the biggest mistake of my life. One I won't be making again."

Then she slipped away and disappeared into the crowd before Jared could tell her that he, too, had fallen in love.

And maybe never really fallen out.

CHAPTER SEVEN

WHAT had Callie been thinking? That she could turn the tables on Jared and not get involved?

That was like diving into the deep end of the pool and expecting to stay dry. Because every time Jared Townsend touched her, every part of her got involved. Very involved.

And she found herself wanting to do a lot more than just make up for breaking his heart all those years ago. She began thinking beyond the next few days. Actually looking down the road. At a future.

And that was the one thing Callie had learned long ago not to do. Because planning a future only meant that all her plans would go awry.

What's more, it scared her. Caught her in the clutches of a fear worse than anything every horror filmmaker in the world could put on the big screen.

She needed to get out of this whole crazy relationship now, while she still could. Jared was a nice guy and it would only be doing him a disservice to let this thing go any further.

"Callie, are you hearing me?"

Callie sighed and returned her attention to the phone call. "Yes, Mom, I am."

"I'll be there in a couple days. I don't have a definite plan. Did I tell you? I ran into an old friend the other day and he invited me down to his beach house in Bermuda. So, anyway, I don't really want to book a hotel or anything in Boston. Surely you can put me up for a day or two when I get there."

"Of course." Callie glanced at the sofa bed, already knowing that would be her bedroom, because she'd give her mother the queen mattress. "Have you talked to Dad lately?"

Silence. "I don't even know that man's phone number anymore."

"He's left town again?"

"I presume so." Her mother paused, and on the other end, Callie could hear her take a sip of something with ice—soda or water. Whatever it was, Callie knew it wouldn't have alcohol. Not anymore. "Why do you care?"

"I don't know," Callie said. "I really don't. I guess I keep wondering why."

Her mother snorted. "I stopped wondering that the third time he walked out on us. And then I filed for divorce instead of looking for him. You're better off forgetting him, Callie. Even if he is your father."

"Don't you ever wonder, though? Where he is? Why he keeps running off?"

"No, I don't. I moved on, as should you. Anyway, they're calling my flight. See you later." Her mother hung up.

Callie replaced the receiver in the phone and fingered the list of phone numbers beside it. All of them for her father, who moved as often as some people changed the television station. He'd moved again, last month, and not bothered to leave a forwarding address.

Eventually her father would call. Tell her where he was. Until then, she'd wonder. Look for him on the street. Just as she had in every city she'd visited, every town she'd been to during the years she'd traveled with Tony. Once, she'd run into him, in Mexico, but before she'd had a chance to talk to him—really talk—he'd been gone. Again.

The clock in the hall chimed the hour and Callie jerked to attention, realizing she'd be late for work. There was something to be said for schedules, for the way one kept her on track.

Most of all, sticking to a schedule gave her something to do and think about, something besides her screwed-up family and Jared

Townsend, who had only added fuel to a fire that was in danger of raging out of control.

"Dude, that's totally you."

Jared cast an unconvinced glance in the mirror outside the dressing room. Teenage boys milled around them, shopping and giving Jared cynical looks. Rock music pounded on the stereo system, its insistent beat seeming to drum home the message that this store was light years away from Jared's usual venue. "I look ridiculous."

"You look like a guy who's actually kind of cool." Pope pointed at the untucked bowling shirt and stonewashed jeans that he'd talked Jared into buying at one of those stores with the odd name that Pope frequented. "Any girl will think you're hot now."

Jared scanned the store's high-school-aged demographic. "Any girl under the age of eighteen."

"Dude, that's like a felony. Don't joke about that." Pope put up his hands, backed up a couple of steps. "It brings up bad memories for me."

"Okay, okay." Jared took one last glance in the mirror. "I still think I look too young. But if you think it's okay—"

Pope pushed him toward the door. "Quit worrying so much and go see your lady."

"She's not my lady, Pope. I'm actually just using her as part of the research. Sort of."

"*Dude*. Why? Wait. Is this some new dating method I haven't thought of?"

"No, no, nothing like that. I'm simply trying to maintain my distance."

Pope stared at him. "You seriously need to get away from that computer. I think it's eating your brain."

"It's not like that, Pope." Jared ducked back into the dressing room, changed into his own clothes and hung the new shirt back on the hanger. Then the two of them walked over to the register. "I simply don't have time in my life for a relationship right now."

"Uh-huh. That's like saying you don't have time to run a virus scan, dude."

Jared arched a brow as he handed over his credit card and the shirt to a tattooed and pierced salesclerk. "Virus scan?"

"Yeah. Dating's a necessity for living. You have to do it on a regular basis or you forget how. Start throwing in that research business and you just confuse everything." Pope waved his hands in a wide, peaceful circle. "Keep it simple, and for Pete's sake, don't put your personal test tube into the company data pool."

A few minutes later, Jared left the store wearing

his new shirt. He pulled his notebook out of his pants pocket and started flipping through the pages. He passed by his To Do list, each item neatly ordered and prioritized. Then he came to his copious pages of couples research.

And then, a series of pages labeled simply Callie.

His observations about her, with him trying to be so objective. But as he read the words he'd written down, he realized not a single sentence had the detached sound of a scientist. Pope was right. Jared was kidding himself if he thought he could keep up the wall of research between them.

Because any wall built with pencils and paper was too damned thin.

Keep it simple, Pope had said. But when had anything ever been simple with Callie?

If he had any brains at all—and those people at the SAT scoring centers had sure thought he did years ago—he'd concentrate on work, not his love life.

Even if that love life kept intruding on his every thought, kept him up at night, had him spending ungodly sums of money in stores he'd never frequented before, all because Callie had commented on his tie and clipboard. For the first time in a long time, Jared was considering stepping outside of the carefully constructed box he'd lived his life by.

Take that risk a second time, with the same

woman. That was about as far from simple as a man could get. And yet, it fired him up in ways he hadn't been in such a long time.

Fine, then. To hell with work. To hell with the research.

A few minutes later, he found himself not at work, but at Callie's doorstep. She opened the door, clearly surprised to see him. "Oh, Jared. I didn't expect to see you."

"I'm sorry for showing up out of the blue, but I wanted to—" He stopped talking, realizing he had no plan. No plan? Jared Townsend never went anywhere or did anything without a plan. It was an odd, but almost liberating feeling. "I just wanted to see you."

She leaned against the doorjamb, about to say something, then her gaze swept over him, and she caught her first sentence and began another. "What are you wearing?"

"Uh…something new."

A smile curved slowly up her face. "Well, it looks nice."

Pope was getting a raise. And a case of beer.

"Thanks." Then he glanced again at her face. A shade dropped over her eyes, her smile gone, spelling something he didn't want to hear, Jared was sure. "If this isn't a good time…" Damn. He should have had a plan. What was he thinking?

"I did want to talk to you—"

"Later," he said, stepping forward, cutting her off. "Let's go down to the beach, Callie. Take a walk, enjoy the day."

She shook her head. "I can't. I have to go to work."

"It's nearly three. Aren't you almost done for the day?"

"There's an emergency with one of our brides. A floral crisis of all things."

Jared laughed. "A floral *crisis?*"

Callie nodded. "She opted to hire an outside florist and he didn't deliver. Literally. Her wedding is in a few hours and she's in a panic, so I need to run to the flower market, get a load of flowers, head over to the Belles office, make up a bunch of arrangements, and get them delivered. All before five."

"Sounds like a lot of work for one woman."

She laughed. "It is. But I've done it before."

"Wouldn't it be more fun with two?" He had a pile of work on his desk. Work he should be getting to, and on any other day, the facts and figures would be interesting, a challenge he'd enjoy.

Except the lithe figure standing before him was ten times more enticing.

She considered him. "You'd help me?"

"Don't I owe you a favor?"

"What favor do you owe me?"

Jared took another step closer, one that allowed him to inhale the floral notes of her perfume, see the golden flecks in her green eyes, catch the hints of sunlight in her hair. "Home ec. Apron making. I sewed my thumb into the seam and you took pity on me." She'd sat at the machine next to him, and that had been the real reason Jared hadn't been able to sew a straight line. Because he'd spent most of the class period watching Callie. Sneaking glances at her hourglass shape, at the way her skirt rose up and exposed a flash of thigh, a curve of calf. He'd asked her dozens of questions about everything from threading needles to working the treadle, just to find an excuse to talk to her.

"I believe you evened the score in Chemistry," Callie said.

"I don't think helping you remember a few elements even comes close to sewing every one of my home ec projects for me."

"I didn't..." Callie thought a second. "Okay, maybe I did."

"And don't forget all the cooking you did in Mrs. Lolly's class, too. I never did master eggs Benedict."

She grinned. "Hollandaise Sauce can be a little tricky."

He stood closer to her now, closer than he'd

been five seconds ago. He watched her inhale, exhale, her every breath even more interesting now as it had been before. When had she ever not been fascinating to him? What was it about Callie Phillips? The edge of recklessness to her? Or the way she seemed to call him on all his bluffs?

"And then there was that term paper in college," he continued. "The one on Lady Macbeth." The one he'd called her about, lying when he'd said he'd never read the play, because he'd spotted her across the campus and realized sometimes God threw second chances at a man.

"I'm sure you could have mastered that, Jared," Callie said, her eyes meeting his. "You were always really smart."

"I couldn't have written that paper, not without you. Not that one or the one on Plato at UMass." She was right. He hadn't needed her help on those papers, but for something deeper. For a connection to normalcy.

He wouldn't have survived a single moment of that freshman year in college if he hadn't had her there, but he didn't say that. Didn't tell her how just knowing she was in the same buildings, a few classrooms away, had kept him sane while the rest of his life at home fell apart.

Nor did he tell her that when his life had truly fallen apart and he'd watched her run off to elope with Tony, he'd had to ditch that college and fly clear across the country, thinking that if he could look at the Pacific Ocean and a whole other beach, an entirely different view of the sun, maybe he'd forget about her.

But he never had. Not for a second.

She moved toward him, her green eyes on his, her hand reaching up, fingers grasping his arm, delicate touch curling around his bicep, making him damned glad he'd listened to Pope and opted for a short-sleeved shirt. He was doubling Pope's raise. Promoting him, first thing in the morning. "You didn't need me to help you."

"Oh, but I did."

She watched his mouth form the words, and her lips parted, then closed. "What are we talking about, Jared?"

"Aprons. Term papers." He touched her chin, turned it up. Memorized the feel of her skin beneath his fingers. "Nothing."

She closed her eyes and a heartbeat passed between them.

"Kiss me," Callie whispered, and that was all he needed, all he'd ever needed.

Jared bent down, and covered Callie's mouth with his own. He tangled his fingers in her hair, the curls soft against his hands, her neck warm to his touch. Her body melted into his, fitting perfectly—

Always fitting perfectly, as if Callie had been made for him, no one else.

How he wanted to believe that. For now, Jared would. For now, Jared would kiss her, would taste Callie and would forget all that had happened before. What would happen tomorrow.

She reached up, her hands flat against his back, pulling him closer, her breasts crushing against his chest, inflaming a desire that had never needed anything more than a whisper to spark. Jared deepened his kiss, his tongue darting in to dance with hers, and she returned the gesture, sweet at first, then sparking into a flame, all Callie.

She was fire in his arms, and he shifted to have more of her, his mind catapulting back nearly a decade, remembering what it had been like to be in her bed, to have her with him for one amazing, incredible night.

His touch roved over her body, hands sliding down her back, over her luscious curves, then back up, traveling a path he knew so well. Had memorized, dreamed of so often over the years. Damn, he'd missed her.

She drew back, then laid her head against his chest. "Oh, Jared, what are we doing?"

"I don't know," he said. Because he really didn't. He'd figure it out later. Or maybe, just figure it out as they went along. Even as he knew he shouldn't put this off, should sound the retreat and fall back on the data—

He didn't.

A flicker of the past ran through him, a dangerous, tempting tightrope.

She sighed. "I have to get to work."

His heart thudded in his chest, and he willed it to slow, to remember that they were standing in her doorway and that hauling her off to her bedroom like a caveman probably wouldn't be a good idea. "Flowers first, then fun later?"

She chuckled. "Something like that."

"Well then, I'll definitely have to help you," he said, pressing one quick kiss to her lips again, unable to resist, "so you have plenty of time for fun."

She tipped her chin to look at him, the tease he loved back in her eyes. "If that's the kind of fun you're talking about, then come with me, Flower Boy."

He took her hand, willing to follow her to Holland and back, if necessary. Especially with that kind of promise waiting at the end of the rose-colored rainbow.

"If that career in research ever falls through, I think you have a second calling in tulips," Callie said, stepping back to admire Jared's handiwork.

The two of them had put together a dozen vase centerpieces featuring bright red tulips, white lilies, grape hyacinths, snow drops and ranunculus. Callie had also put together a long table arrangement to run down the bridal banquet table, and created matching corsages and boutonnieres for the wedding party. She put the finishing touches on the bride's crescent bouquet, then gave Jared a high-five. "You're pretty good at this."

He grinned. "I had a good teacher. But don't let this get back to the guys in the lab or I'll never live it down."

"What, flower designing is less manly than doing research for 'A Hundred Questions To Ask Your Honey In The Bedroom?' or whatever the game is that you're designing?"

"Definitely. Sex research is way more cool." He flexed a bicep beneath his new shirt. "See how cool I look now?"

She laughed. "Last I checked, you weren't getting very far in your sex research."

"Take me home and we'll see how far I get."

She slugged him, sending a couple of tulips tumbling to the floor. "You are turning into quite the incorrigible man."

"All your fault. I was a respectable, tie-wearing, clipboard-carrying research scientist before you came back into my life." He picked up the flowers, then came around behind Callie to place them back on the workbench. Her heart raced, every fiber of her painfully aware of Jared behind her, of the heat of his body, so close. "You have ruined me," he whispered in her ear.

"Well, good," she said back, intending to sound flip, to keep treating this like a game.

Only it had stopped being a game somewhere during that kiss back at her apartment. Something had shifted between them and turned what she'd thought had been a moment of levity into something far more serious.

Something Callie hadn't been prepared to handle. Before he'd arrived, she'd been planning to end their relationship, to go back to being just friends. After all, she'd accomplished her goal. She'd wanted to make up for the way she'd broken up with Jared in college, maybe up-end his research plans a little, but now, there was a decided edge between them—

An edge that had taken their relationship to a whole new level. One she couldn't ignore or dismiss.

The kind of level that spelled permanence. Settling down.

Because she knew Jared. He was a white picket fence, golden retriever, hang your name on the door knocker kind of guy all the way.

Callie lived as far from that as possible. She'd grown up in a family that had disintegrated into chaos, and like a couch potato who'd found his sweet spot on the sofa, she knew that topsy-turvy world better than the one Jared came from. Callie had seen too often how wrong "happily ever after" could go, and even though she made her living at tying all those kinds of happy endings up with a pretty bow and a daisy, she didn't believe for a second that the same could work for her.

Even if, for a moment, a tiny part of her had wanted that very same thing, like a child hoping for a pony on Christmas.

"What's wrong?" Jared said. "You got tense all of a sudden."

"I, ah, just need to get these arrangements over to the Henry wedding. If I don't hurry, I'll be late." She grabbed two of the filled vases and turned toward the door.

"Here, let me help you."

"No, I'm fine—"

"Callie—" He moved at the same time as her, and they collided, flowers knocking heads, arrangements tumbling to the floor in a gush of water, Oasis floral foam, floral stems and asparagus fern fronds.

"Oh, no!" Callie dropped to her knees and began grabbing the stems, scooping up everything that she could, trying to salvage the ruined flowers, but the delicate petals had already bruised.

Jared bent down beside her, laying one hand over hers. "Callie. Callie, it's okay."

"No, it's not, you don't understand. It's not okay. It's ruined. Everything's ruined."

"It's only two arrangements. We had plenty of flowers and vases left over. We can make two more in a few minutes. Don't worry. It'll be fine."

But she kept grabbing at the ruined pieces on the floor, her vision blurred, no longer seeing the mess before her, but still trying to pick it up all the same. "No, it won't be. You don't understand. It'll all be ruined."

"Callie." Jared stopped her, his hand on top of hers, his voice louder now, more authoritative. "Look at me."

Finally she did. She swiped at her eyes, then looked up. He hauled her to her feet, then grabbed a tissue and wiped away the rest of her tears.

"What's really wrong?" he asked. "This is about way more than some flowers."

She shook her head. "I have to get to work. The Henry wedding—"

"We have time, so stop avoiding me and tell me what's the matter."

"I can't do this, Jared," she said, her heart hammering in her chest. He was so close, too close, and everything he wanted seemed to overwhelm her as much as the work on her desk, the deadline ticking away. "I can't—"

"We can make another arrangement. Heck, we already made more than a dozen, what's two more?"

"It's not that, it's—" But she couldn't finish. She shot to her feet and went to work, assembling the pieces for another set of centerpieces, grabbing two water-soaked squares of Oasis and shoving them into a second pair of squat silver bowls, then quickly shearing the floral stems into points, reinforcing them by wire-wrapping them to wooden sticks, jabbing them into the foam, arranging them in the same pattern as before.

Jared watched her work, silent for a moment, simply handing her whatever would come next. "Are you going to talk to me about this?"

No. No way. "Stress, that's all."

"Uh-huh. You're about as good a liar as I am a singer."

"I need some of that crimson ribbon."

Jared sliced off the right length, handed it to her, but wouldn't let her change the subject. "Did I do something wrong?"

"No." She sighed. "Yes."

"What?"

She laid down the bow in her hands and turned to face him. "You want too much out of me."

"I haven't said I want anything."

"I can read it in your eyes, in the way you kiss me. In everything between us. It's always been there, Jared. That…expectation. You're not the kind of man who enters into anything lightly."

"And you're suddenly the kind of woman who only has flings? One-night stands?"

"I don't want anything serious. I probably should have told you this from the beginning. I don't want to get married again. I never really did."

"This from the woman who makes her living working on weddings?"

She walked away from the bench, pacing the room, trying to find the words that would explain the push-pull running through her, the fear that overcame her every time she thought about getting close to someone again. "I don't want to take that risk, not a second time."

Jared caught her arm, then her gaze. "Not all men are like Tony."

Her green eyes sought his; the connection filled not with heat this time, but with a need for trust, for reassurance. He wondered if he should have pushed this, should have even said all that he had.

What if they took this to the next level and once again, some man came along and stole Callie's heart right out from under Jared? Some man who was more exciting, more her speed? More the kind of dashing, exciting, rock-and-roll sort of man she went for?

Who was he fooling? A change of clothes, a few minutes on a stage, even a pair of contact lenses, didn't change who he was, didn't put him into the same league as some guy with a swagger and a motorcycle. It never had and it never would.

That, he realized, was probably what she'd been trying to tell him all day. Wasn't that what his research had shown him? Sparks flew—as they had years before between Callie and Tony—and people stopped thinking logically.

Why hadn't he been smart and stuck to his facts and figures instead of delving into a story where he already knew the ending?

"I know not all guys are like Tony," Callie said. "But—"

"But if that's the kind of guy you want," Jared said, the words having a bitter tint to them, as he bit them off, spitting them out before she could. He backed up and released her, turning his attention back to the floral arrangements. He didn't have any idea what the hell to do with the tulips, not without Callie's help, but he made a stab at it anyway. It was far better than hearing her say "Yeah, Tony's the sort of man I want."

"These are done," Callie said, attaching the bows and picking up the arrangements. "I better get them delivered."

"Wait," Jared said, before she could turn away again. "I want to see one more thing."

"What?"

He put down the ribbon in his hands, turned Callie toward him and kissed her, firm and strong, and with everything he had. She responded in an instant, just as heated as she had earlier.

No, he hadn't imagined a second of it. She *did* want him, regardless of anything she had said. But were there enough sparks?

Jared ended the kiss as quickly as it began, a fierce, fast, summer storm. "That's all." He tipped her chin, studying the eyes that he had known most of his life and decided that she may prefer the kind of man that he wasn't, but he was damned if he was going to let her get away this time before he could show her that the professor had a lot to offer, too. He'd made the mistake of giving her up without a fight once before—

And he wasn't going to do it again.

"I've decided," Jared said, "that I need a lot more of that in my life."

"A lot more kissing?" Confusion reigned in her eyes.

"Yeah. And for your information, I'm not

looking to get married right now, either. Maybe down the road, yes. But I'm strictly a living by the seat of my pants guy right now."

She arched a brow. "You? *Really.*"

"Yeah. I started with the shirt, the Tilt-A-Whirl and the elephant ears. Now I want to move on to bigger things." He nodded, cementing the resolution and the idea that maybe there was a way to win Callie again—and prove that nice guys could finish first in her heart. It would mean disproving one of his own theories, but perhaps even the research could be wrong. "And since you seem to be the expert in that area, how about tonight we do something else fun? A little wild even?"

"Jared, I—"

He put a finger over her lips, his pulse quickening with the desire to kiss her again. "No objections. And no expectations beyond tonight, contrary to whatever you *think* you might be reading in my lips and my eyes."

"That's all you want?"

"Yes." He might not be able to sing, but Jared could pull off the occasional white lie. He knew Callie and knew if he pushed her too far in the direction of something serious, she'd run from him faster than an Olympic athlete. "So why don't you stop arguing with me and just have a good time, Callie?"

Finally she smiled, too, and he knew he had won her over again. "I don't know about wild, but if you want a good time tonight, then find yourself a suit and meet me at the Lantana in an hour. And wear your dancing shoes."

CHAPTER EIGHT

CRAZY.

She had to be crazy. Callie rarely attended client weddings, not for lack of invitation, but because for one, showing up at a clearly couple oriented event as a single woman wasn't exactly fun and for another, there were only so many dewy-eyed brides and goofy-grinned grooms she wanted to see in a week. She loved working with them, creating their floral arrangements and bouquets, but there was something about being at the actual wedding and reception that reminded her of how she had failed in her own marriage.

So, she did her best to avoid the events, begging off whenever Belle or Serena or any of the other women asked her to go.

Which explained Belle's nearly measurable shock when Callie walked into the Henry reception, with Jared on her arm. "Has hell frozen over, darlin', or are pigs fallin' from the sky out there?"

"Neither." Callie smoothed a hand over her dress, and gave Belle a grin. "I was in the mood for a little dancing. That's all."

Belle gave her a knowing smile, then another, bigger smile when she glimpsed Jared beside her. "Uh-huh. And I see you brought along quite the dancin' partner, too. Who is this nice young man?"

Callie made the introductions. She could see that Belle took to Jared immediately, impressed with his easy charm and quick smile. Soon, they were chatting like old friends, with Belle learning most of Jared's history in ten minutes.

"I approve," Belle whispered in Callie's ear. "He's a catch and a half."

"Oh, he's not—"

"Well, he should be. Now, you two get out there and dance," Belle said, then gave Callie's hand a quick squeeze and headed off to attend to the wedding party.

The band started playing a Frank Sinatra song, sending several couples swinging onto the dance floor. Above them, lights twinkled from the ballroom ceiling, which had been hung with cream-colored shantung silk. The bride's family had spared no expense, and Callie was glad she had opted for one of the fancier dresses in her closet.

"Shall we?" Jared asked, putting out his hand. She inhaled, taking a second look at him. Belle had been right. Jared did indeed make for an attractive dancing partner. He wore a tailored navy suit that seemed custom made for him, the white shirt and red tie ordinary on any other man, but with Jared's dark hair and even with his glasses, he looked almost dashing. He had a way of carrying a suit, perhaps because he was accustomed to being in business clothes, that gave him an air of handsomeness and authority. And made Callie's pulse skitter.

"Are you a better dancer than you are a singer?" she asked, teasing.

"Try me and see."

The deep baritone of his voice sent a thrill running through her. A challenge, a dare, almost. She knew she should say no, should resist him, because every time she got close to him, her plan to simply make up for that one moment in college—and to end it now, before anyone got in too deep, and worse, got hurt—seemed to go off track and spiral into something far, far more profound.

But Jared's hand in hers was warm, the music tempting, the look in his eyes so...

Irresistible.

Jared kept surprising her. Especially today, when he'd kissed her—twice—with fire in his veins. That kiss still had her reeling. But he'd also surprised her when he'd told her he wasn't looking for anything serious.

Could it be that she had read him wrong? That he wasn't the homebody and Mr. Traditional that she'd always thought? A flicker of disappointment ran through her, which was insane. This was, after all, what she wanted, wasn't it?

A man who wouldn't expect anything out of her. Who wouldn't pressure her to make any commitments, to put down any roots.

"If we're going to dance," she said to Jared now, stepping into his arms, forgetting the internal war, "then we're really going to dance."

He grinned. "That sounds like a challenge."

"If you're up to it."

"Hey, don't let the tie fool you. I'm a real Twinkle Toes underneath the pinstripe."

She laughed so hard she nearly tripped. "Is that your secret? Keep telling me jokes so I won't notice that you're out of step?"

Jared's palm went to her back, his other hand slipped under hers and he spun her into a space between an older couple and another, younger couple who were engaged in a hug clench.

Oh, he was most definitely in step. With every beat of her pulse, too.

Callie hardly noticed the blur of pastels, suits and tuxedos, the bride standing on the sidelines, greeting her guests, or the other Belles watching her and chatting with Belle. The only thing she felt or noticed was the feel of Jared's touch, like an iron against her back, hot against her skin, even through the satin of her dress, that she leaned into it slightly, craving more.

"My plan," he said, "is to completely sweep you off your feet and dazzle you so much, you won't want to let go."

He'd already done that. She didn't want to let go. Didn't want *him* to let go.

She was treading on more than his toes right now—she was hitting dangerous, scary territory. The kind that led to a broken heart. Hadn't she already been down that path once before?

And learned that her instincts where men were concerned were about as reliable as a broken light-bulb?

"Relax," Jared said, his breath warm against her ear.

She did, nearly going liquid in his arms, unable to resist the sound of his voice, the romantic melody of the song, and the hum of romance carrying all around them.

"How did you get to be such a good dancer?" she asked.

"My mother insisted on Arthur Murray when I was a kid."

"Really?" Callie arched a brow. "Why?"

A muscle twitched in Jared's jaw. "To keep me busy and out of the house every Tuesday and Thursday afternoon from three to five."

"Were you one of those troublemaker kids?" As soon as the joke left Callie's mouth, she regretted it, because she sensed a tightening in Jared's arms, a tension that hadn't been there before.

"She was having an affair with the next door neighbor's husband. If I was home, I'd tell my father."

Her heart broke for him in that instant, and she wanted to go back in time, make it up to him somehow. "I had no idea, Jared. I'm sorry."

He shrugged. "That's okay. I'm over it."

But Callie knew, because she'd gone through a childhood marked by trouble and constant upheaval, that you never really get over it, just wore it like a scar. How much had he locked inside himself, the secrets he'd held to his chest, just like she had, always maintaining the facade of a happy family?

"But that had to be terrible." She thought of how quiet he'd been in high school, how he'd kept to himself, never letting on about anything going wrong at home. No wonder they'd become friends. They were each survivors, of a sort, only children in families that redefined dysfunction. She slipped closer to him, laid her head on his shoulder. "I understand that kind of family."

He didn't say anything for a long time, just danced with her, and she could feel the tension ebb a bit at a time, one note after another. "It was never easy," Jared said softly. "Makes trust a little hard."

"I know what you mean. My father was the one who had trouble sticking around."

Jared kept her close, as if soothing her. "Then I'm sorry, too."

She smiled. "I grew up to be reasonably well-adjusted and normal. Just like you."

He chuckled a little. "I vowed when I finally fell in love that I would never cheat, never be untrue. And that's the real reason why I'm still not married."

She drew back to look at him, to connect with those clear blue eyes of the man she'd known most of her life. "I don't understand."

"Because if I'm going to give my heart to someone and settle down, I want to be sure I can do it right. No ifs, ands or buts." His gaze met hers, intense and deep, the lightness of the afternoon's conversation gone. "When I commit to something, Callie, I give it a hundred percent, and I expect the same in return."

Callie swallowed hard and pressed her cheek back to his shoulder. She shouldn't have been surprised. The Jared she knew was exactly that kind of man. He wasn't the wild man he'd pretended he wanted to be. Heck, he didn't even cross onto wild man streets.

He hadn't changed at all. Somehow, that satisfied her, gave her comfort, like knowing the same store would always be on the same corner, and carry the same inventory. But now, she'd seen that store had something extra, a little something special behind its doors.

True, full-force commitment.

Where she, on the other hand, had never stayed around long enough to give anyone or anything a hundred percent. Except for Tony, and he'd gone and thrown her commitment away as easily as a used tissue.

"Well, you got the Belle seal of approval," Callie said, changing the subject to one that was less serious and as far from commitments and permanence as she could take it. "That's about as good as it gets around here."

"And what about the Callie seal of approval?" Jared asked. "How am I doing in that department?"

"Fine," she said, trying to keep her tone as light as her steps.

Jared tipped her chin to meet his gaze. "Really?"

The song ended and Callie stepped out of his touch. "I should get something to drink. It's hot in here."

Hot between them, hot in the room. A lot of things suddenly bubbling to the surface, and Callie needed space. She spun away before Jared could catch up to her, blending into the crowd. Her heart thundered in her chest, her mind a whirlwind of emotion and racing thoughts. Jared had become more than what she'd expected, and she needed a moment to process it all.

At the bar, she ran into Serena, who had taken a seat at the far end. The usually cheerful blonde's face had a downturned cast to it. Immediately Callie's focus turned to her friend. "Hey, Serena, you okay?"

"Oh, yeah, sure."

But everything in Serena's voice said otherwise. Callie still held some doubts. "If you need me, I'm here, you know."

"I'm fine. Tired." Serena toyed with her wineglass, then gestured at the busy reception. "This turned out to be a really nice wedding. The flowers are gorgeous, Callie. You always do an amazing job, even last minute."

"Look who's talking. I love the dress you designed." Callie glanced over her shoulder at the bride, who wore an elegant sheath dress with an empire bodice beaded in a filigree pattern. Silvery ribbon trimmed the flounced train, a perfect offset to the satin sheen of the fabric. "And thank you again for helping to talk Marsha Schumacher out of a fuchsia wedding dress."

Serena laughed. "That would have been a disaster. I convinced her to limit her pink to some beading and a little ribbon along the hemline. She's going all out with a sweetheart gown, a full skirt and a train that's going to take ten minutes to make its journey down the aisle. That, I told her, would make enough of a statement."

Callie chuckled. "That's Marsha for you. It'll be one of our more interesting weddings."

"Speaking of interesting," Serena said. "Who's that man you're with? Is he the one you told us about at the poker game?"

Callie swallowed and faced the truth that she had been ignoring for days. Five seconds ago, it had just slapped her in the face, in Jared's last few words. All these years, karma had thrown them together again and again, and she'd missed the freeway sign—until now. "He is. And I think… Audra was right. I might have just found one of the last few Mr. Rights on the planet."

"Mr. Right?" Serena's jaw dropped. "You? The big cynic?"

"Don't tell the others. They'll never let me live

it down. But…" Callie turned and glanced over her shoulder at Jared, who had stopped to talk to Belle. The two of them were engaged in some kind of conversation that had them both laughing and when Callie looked at him, she recognized the feeling in her gut.

She'd only felt it twice before. Once with Tony. And once with Jared.

On Halloween night. In college.

Only this time, with Jared, the feeling was ten times stronger than she'd ever felt before. She wanted to burst out of her skin, shout to the world, sing along with the band. Smile, dance…

"Serena, I think I'm falling in love with him."

"You're kidding me, right? You, the one who is so commitment-shy, you'd have to be duct-taped to a chair to even talk about marrying again?"

Callie nodded and laughed, feeling lighter than she had in weeks. Months. Maybe even years. What had happened in the last few hours? She'd gone from thinking she needed to end it with Jared to realizing—

He was a man who was committed to commitment.

And wasn't that, in the end, really, what any woman wanted? A man who would love her and be true. Maybe that was what Callie had needed to keep her from running scared. "It seems that

Mr. Nice is actually very, very right for me," she said.

Serena raised her glass of wine in Callie's direction. "Cheers to you."

Still, something in Serena's voice fell flat and Callie returned her attention to her friend. "Everything okay with Rupert?" she asked again.

Serena bit her lip and glanced away. "Yes." She drew in a breath. "No." Then she spun back to face Callie. "But don't say anything to anyone. I'm sure this is just a momentary thing we're going through and we'll work it out. I don't want to spoil Julie's excitement over getting engaged and Audra's wedding this weekend. Everyone's all excited about those things and if they find out Rupert and I are having a little—" she paused "—fight…they'll feel like they have to pause in their happiness to comfort me and I don't want that. So will you keep it quiet? Not say anything?"

"Sure." Callie had the feeling that there was more than a small fight going on between Serena and Rupert. That made her pause for a moment. If Serena—the one who'd always had the most unshakable faith in Mr. Right—was having problems with her perfect man, then what did that mean about Callie's future with Jared? Could Callie's instincts be wrong again?

Serena laid a hand on Callie's arm. "I think your

guy is great. And you seemed really happy on the dance floor. You *deserve* to be happy, Callie. Please don't let me dampen your mood. Go prove us all wrong and find Mr. Right." Serena grinned, the moment of melancholy erased.

"Is that a challenge?" Callie asked, echoing Audra's dare from earlier in the week.

"I'll stake my next poker hand on it."

"You're on." She gave Serena a smile, then headed back in Jared's direction. Willing to take that chance—

Even as it took her breath away.

"Can I steal him away from you?" Callie said when she reached Jared.

Belle laughed. "Certainly, darlin'." She gave Callie a smile, then shared the smile with Jared. "Take care of her, now."

"I will, ma'am."

"I'm sure you will. You seem the type." Belle paused, listening for a second as one of the other members of the Wedding Belles spoke to her through the wireless headphones the women used to communicate during a wedding. "They're about to cut the cake, so I better head over there. You enjoy yourself, Callie. The rest of us have it under control. And if I'm lucky, there'll be a piece of Natalie's cake left over for me."

After Belle headed toward the cake table, Callie

caught Jared's hand. "Do you want to watch them cut the cake?"

"Actually I'd like to catch some air. It's really warm in here."

"Sounds like a good idea." Being alone with him sounded like the best idea of the night, in fact. With Jared leading the way, they slipped outside. A few guests milled outside, the couples huddled together, sharing a quiet moment by the elegant outdoor water fountain. Two of the ushers were laughing and tying cans on the bride and groom's car.

Jared and Callie circled around the building, strolling along the brick pathway. The sun had set, bathing the landscaped grounds in moonlight, giving the venue an intimate air. The music from the band drifted through the open windows, providing a soft undertow of harmony. "It's a gorgeous evening."

"It is," Jared agreed, drawing her to him.

She grinned. "You're not talking about the weather, are you?"

He shook his head. "Nope." He leaned down, brushed his lips against hers and everything within Callie hummed like the music drifting on the evening breeze.

Why had she never really seen how good Jared was before? Why hadn't she been smart years ago and thrown Tony aside, choosing Jared instead? Why had she opted for the one man who had done nothing but break her heart?

Maybe she was, as her mother had often told her, a slow learner when it came to things like this. Either way, Jared was here now, and so was she, and that was enough. And perfect.

Perfect…except for the dropping temperature.

"It's chilly," Callie said, wishing she'd worn a dress with sleeves. She turned into Jared and slid her arms under his jacket, seeking the warmth of Jared's body. Leaning into him, feeling happy for the first time in so long. So very long. And thinking maybe all those fairy tales she'd helped make come true weren't really fictionalized stories but actual realities—

A reality she, too, could have.

"You know, we're at a wedding, a perfect place to do the rest of those interviews you need to do. It seems you keep forgetting about your research." She snuggled closer, Jared drawing her in, laying a soft kiss on the top of her head.

"That's because you distract me."

"Mmm. And I'm not about to apologize, not while I'm getting warm." As she moved, her arm jostled something on the inside pocket of his jacket, and before she could catch it, the item had slipped past the silky fabric of his jacket and the satin of her dress, then fallen with a soft kerplat onto the ground.

"Whoops. I'm sorry," Callie said, spinning and bending to grab it.

"No, let me—"

They reached for the flash of white on the ground at the same time, but Callie was quicker, her hand grasping the small object before she realized what it was. The handwriting, the sentences processing through her mind, the numbers jumbling together with the words, all of it twisting from a puzzle—

Into one clear conclusion.

No. It couldn't be. Not Jared. He wouldn't.

But he had.

Callie held the notebook, staring at it for a long moment, then looked up at Jared, her mouth opened in a question.

"Callie, let me explain."

"This has my name on it. Notes about me."

"It's for my research. Part of the notes I was taking for Wiley."

"*I* was a part of your research? Part of your hypothesis? You were taking notes on *me?*" Hurt rocketed through her body, searing her heart, racing across her veins, tearing her apart as surely as a shredder. Still, she stared at the words, disbelieving. "You were using me?"

"No, it wasn't like that, I swear. I mean, it started out like that, in a way, but—"

She flipped through the pages, reading Jared's familiar tight scrawl. His notations about her reactions to him. Her words. Her every step, every breath, every kiss. Every inflection. "I was nothing more than a rat in your maze."

She'd been wrong. So wrong.

The disappointment hurtled to the pit of her stomach like a boulder. She stumbled back, the notebook falling from her hands, tumbling to the ground in a flutter of white, like dove's wings.

"Callie, I had no intention of hurting you. I only wanted to try to figure out what made you tick so I could—"

"So you could use it against me." She shook her head, putting up her hands, not wanting to hear any more. "Don't even try to sugarcoat this, Jared. You and your logic, your hypotheses, your plans. I'm not an experiment. I'm a flesh and blood woman. You keep talking to me about taking risks." She gestured toward the pile of papers on the floor. "Well that's not about taking risks. That's about planning a love life. For a man who supposedly knows everything there is to know about relationships, you are as dumb as they come."

Then she spun on her heel and walked away.

CHAPTER NINE

CALLIE stood by the altar, glancing from the groomsmen to the priest, then to the bridesmaids, knowing something was horribly wrong. The church was full of friends and family, the pews beautifully decorated with twin pink roses tied with pale blue satin bows. Simple, tasteful, elegant. The white runner had been scattered with rose petals, the organist had played the entire round of wedding music in her repertoire, and at the other end of the church, behind closed doors, the bride waited.

But the groom had yet to show.

An empty place marked where he was to stand. The priest looked from one side of the church to the other, as if the bridal party would explain the missing man. "Where is he?" Regina whispered to Callie.

"I have no idea. Do you think he's with Audra?" Callie glanced at the other women, who all shrugged, and sent worried glances down the bridesmaid line that said they had no idea, either.

"He better be," Regina said. "Either that or kidnapped by aliens, because there's no excuse to do this to her."

The people in the church shifted in their seats, then began to talk, the nervous hum of speculation carrying like a virus from pew to pew. Dread curled around Callie. Something had gone wrong. She knew it.

"I'll be back. Try not to look panicked," she whispered to Regina, then she headed down the aisle, knowing the quick disappearance of a bridesmaid toward the vestibule would only hasten the wagging of tongues. But Audra was in trouble—Callie was sure of it—and she didn't care what the guests thought.

She slipped through the double doors of the church. "Audra?"

"O-o-over here."

Callie followed the sound of Audra's voice and found her friend sitting on the stairs that led to the church balcony. Her dress had puddled around her, the simple crepe and chiffon design now wrinkled. Her handheld bouquet of cream and pale pink roses sat on the stairs beside her, seeming to droop, as if commiserating with her. "What's wrong?"

Audra looked up, her face marred by tears. "He's not coming."

"Oh, hon. He's just late. He'll be here."

Audra shook her head. "Callie, I'm a logical person. I should have seen this coming. David's been…distant lately. It was as if he didn't care about the wedding. I had this bad feeling when I woke up this morning and then—" She waved a hand toward the church doors. "I should have looked at the probabilities of this happening and known."

"Audra, who can predict this kind of thing? And really, he could still—"

"Callie, he's not coming." Audra's voice broke on the last word, and Callie surged forward, drawing her friend into a hug. As she did, she felt five other pairs of arms joining in, firm and secure, as comforting as a blanket. Serena, Natalie, Julie, Regina and Belle.

The Wedding Belles, there for each other. As they always had been. The women pulled together, a sea of bridesmaids in soft blue satin halter dresses, hugging and crying as if it were their wedding, their missing groom. After a while, Audra pulled back, swiped at her face. "You all are the best. I don't know what I'd do without you. Thank you."

"Darlin', if I see that boy, I'll shoot him for you," Belle said.

Audra laughed. "You don't need to do that. Just send him all the bills for the wedding."

"Done." Belle grinned. "Anything else you want us to do?"

"Could you guys go in and tell everyone? I can't face…" Audra's voice trailed off.

The rest of the Belles nodded. "We'll do it. Then I say we go to the reception and have one hell of a party on David's dime. After all, the coq au vin is already cooked, Natalie made a great cake and we're all dressed up." Callie drew her friends together. "What do you say, Audra?"

Audra bit her lip, then rose, her face determined. "Okay. But let me change first. If I'm going to party," she said, a grin curving up her lips, "I'm going to put on some jeans."

"That's the Audra we know." One more hug, and then the Belles were ready to face anything again.

After the last song had been played, all of Natalie's white chocolate raspberry cake had been eaten and Belle had plopped into a chair, exhausted, Callie finally had a moment to breathe.

And deal with what happened last night with Jared. How could she have been so stupid? Trusted him so completely? She glanced over at Audra, the one who thought everything through, added everything up in her columns, made all the numbers balance, and realized that if someone like Audra could be wrong, then what made Callie think she could get it right?

Clearly the thought that there was a Mr. Right for everyone was crazy.

Callie glanced back at her friends, who had settled down around one of the tables. They were laughing, Audra's face finally cheery again.

Callie should join them. Return to that inner circle. But a part of her held back, the part that operated on a long-held protective instinct. Staying too long, wrapping herself up too tight with anyone led to hurt. She'd already been here for three years, the longest she'd ever lived anywhere since her childhood.

If she stayed, she'd always have Jared in her backyard. A few blocks away. A heartbreak right around the corner. Callie closed her eyes and leaned against the wall. In her mind, she pictured a beach. A solitary hut, far from people, from Jared.

An escape.

Surely that would be better than staying here and waiting—waiting to be hurt all over again.

"Dude, you are seriously one clue short of *Jeopardy*," Pope said when he entered the office and took one look at Jared's attire for the day. He shook his head. "Did you learn nothing from me?"

Jared refused to enter into an argument about his reversion to a button-down shirt and tie. The whole foray into a youthful look had gone awry and he wasn't going back there. "I'm not trying to impress anyone. I'm just trying to do my job."

"Yeah, and how's that going? You hate this place."

"So?" Jared scowled, turned away from Pope and went back to entering the data into the computer. He intended to bury himself in work until the project was done. That was a lot easier than thinking about how everything with Callie had gone so wrong the other night. She hadn't returned any of his calls, hadn't been home any of the times he'd been on her doorstep, and if she'd been at the Wedding Belles office either of the times he'd stopped by, she'd been hiding. So far, Callie had disappeared off the face of the earth.

He'd sent flowers. Two cards. Left voice mails. Done everything he could think of to apologize. But since romance wasn't exactly his strong suit— maybe he should open up a few of the games that lay around the Wiley Games building—he had yet to achieve a response from her.

So instead he'd buried himself in his work, interviewing couple after couple, working his way down the list he'd gotten from Callie earlier in the week. He'd sat in restaurants and bars listed as "hot spots" in the local newspapers, clipboard in hand, seeking interview subjects. Basically, not having any love life but plenty of statistical time.

Jared sighed. "You're right. I'm working hard, but I'm not happy about it."

"So, quit working here, dude. Find some big think tank or brain pool where they throw all the brainiacs into a room and solve world hunger or something."

"I tried that. There's no money in it."

"Blah-blah-blah," Pope said. "I think you're just scared."

Jared wheeled around. "Did you just call me scared?"

"Well, yeah. Buddy, you are working here, developing *bedroom* games, for Pete's sake. I'm embarrassed to tell my *dog* I work here. You're the one with all the letters after your name. How do you wake up in the morning and come into this place?"

"It's a paycheck," Jared muttered.

"You could do better."

"Yeah, I could, but—" Jared cut off the sentence.

"But what?" Pope leaned forward, his arms over the back of the chair, his legs, as always, draped over the sides. "But the sky is gonna fall in if you quit, Chicken Little?"

"Hey, that's not even a nice thing to say."

"And that's your biggest problem," Pope said, pointing at Jared, as if he'd just hit the lottery. "You are too *nice*. I heard you talking to the boss yesterday, being all nice when he asked you to work late. He asked me to work late and I told him, 'Later, dude, I got a date.' You know what he told me?"

Jared sighed. "I have no idea. He docked your pay?"

"He said, 'Okay. Make up the time another day then.'"

"I'm doing my job, Pope. There's nothing wrong with that."

"Yeah, there is. When you should be working at a better job. One that actually uses more than three of your brain cells."

Jared scowled. "You're not my mother, or my boss, so let it go."

Pope leaned forward and dropped the classified ads onto Jared's desk. An ad for a position with a Boston think tank had been circled in red. "Go forth and apply, my friend. That's the kind of place where you belong. Not in this rat maze."

Jared shoved the paper to the side. "Pope, I have a deadline to meet."

"You *are* scared. What, did you get burned by the research gods or something?"

"Something like that." Jared wasn't about to talk about it. Not now, not ever.

"It's your funeral," Pope said, getting to his feet. "Your boring, dead-end funeral. I'm going down the hall for a caffeine fix. Want anything?"

Jared shook his head. Pope left the room, leaving Jared to enter the research he'd compiled for the game into the computer. Research that, really, meant nothing, not if Jared didn't turn it into something meaningful. Actually do something more than create a little couples' fun with the statistics he'd compiled.

Meaning take a chance, step outside his comfort zone. Pope was right. Jared did hate the job. He'd give anything to work at a place like what Pope had circled in the newspaper.

Jared stopped typing, read the ad and considered the position. Years ago, that would have been the kind of job he'd have taken in a heartbeat. It had, in fact, been the kind of job he'd had. The kind of career he'd been fast-tracking along, until his life had crossed over and put a stop to a career that came with anything without regular hours, a paycheck that didn't depend on research grants.

"Catch," Pope said.

Jared spun and put out his hands, catching the cola just as it sailed across the room, narrowly missing his monitor. "You could have wiped out my computer, or I could have missed. You live on the edge, Pope."

Pope grinned. "Only way to go."

Jared popped the top, took a long sip, then leaned back in his chair and put his feet up on the desk. "Why?"

"Why what?"

"Why are you the way you are? Why do you skate on the edge of life? Take risks with your job, your relationships, your choice in clothing?"

Pope looked down at his concert T-shirt, the opened button shirt he wore over it and his multi-pocketed khakis. "*This* is a fashion statement."

"Yeah, that's what I'd call it, too, if I was being polite." Jared snorted, then took another drink from the can. He'd leaned back in the chair, stretching the kinks out of his neck. He had spent too many hours here.

"Dude, you only live once," Pope said. "I don't see any point in doing anything other than living as large and loud as possible. What have I got to lose? My reputation?" Pope snorted. "Hell, I lost that years ago. My job? There's always another one. My girlfriend? Well, isn't fighting for the woman you love half the fun?"

"I thought you didn't believe in committed relationships."

Pope shrugged and Jared could swear he saw a blush rise in Pope's cheeks. "Ah, that's part of the act. You can't be cool if you're running around spouting love sonnets and talking about wanting babies and a Labrador. I have an image to protect."

"You're a softie."

"I prefer the term well-rounded modern man," Pope said, puffing out his chest, "but…yeah. What about you? How are things going with your lady?"

Jared let out a breath. "Let's just say my career is on a faster track than my relationship."

"Whoa, dude, that's not good. You try jewelry? Flowers? Dropping to your knees and begging like a dog?"

"I don't think any of that's going to work." Jared tapped on his computer screen, indicating the facts and figures he'd been working on all morning. "She found out I'd been tabulating some of her responses for the research project."

Pope wagged a finger at him and sat back against his chair. "That is so not you, Doc. Involving people you know in a research project, tampering with the results by getting personally involved. Not a good idea. What were you thinking?"

"That was the problem. I was thinking too much." Jared rose, pacing the room, realizing that the very thing he had prized the most about himself turned out to be his biggest issue. "I didn't want to fall for Callie again and so I decided to keep this wall up between us. I used the only wall I knew, and it was stupid, because she found out and ended things with us."

Pope shook his head. "Man, you've definitely spent too much time cooped up with the lab rats. You became one yourself."

Jared laughed. "Yeah, I did."

Pope crossed to him and laid a hand on his shoulder, his face somber, looking as sage as Solomon's. "There's only one thing to do."

"What's that?"

Pope pointed to the newspaper. "First, get out of the maze while you still can. And when you do, head straight for Downtown Crossing."

"Downtown Crossing? Why?"

Pope grinned. "That's the diamond district, my friend. You want to start living on the edge? Blow your last paycheck down there, then head right on over to your lady's house and give her an apology she'll never forget. Preferably one made up of two carats or more." Pope nodded, then walked to the exit, pausing in the doorway. "Take it from one who knows. There's not a woman in the world who can say no to an offer like that."

CHAPTER TEN

RIGHT now, Callie hoped she'd never see another engagement or wedding again.

After the debacle at Audra's wedding, and the horrible ending to the Henry wedding, not to mention her own bad experience with the whole process—

Callie was done. Done with anything remotely reminding her of "I do".

Mr. Right did not exist, not in her world. Apparently that message hadn't made it over to Marsha Schumacher, however, who was still happily planning her all-pink, all-the-time wedding.

Callie caught Regina's eye over the table set up in the ballroom and exchanged twin restrained looks of impatience. They'd already been there for a half an hour, waiting while Marsha underwent the most important debate of the century.

Over her champagne glasses.

"I don't know," Marsha said. She tipped her head left, then right. "I still can't decide."

They'd been standing in the ballroom for a half an hour, while Marsha considered swan-patterned crystal champagne flutes over heart-patterned flutes, neither decision which Callie or Regina needed to be a part of, but Marsha and her mother had insisted the wedding planners stay because they needed additional "professional stemware input," regardless of the extra cost for the opinions.

"Whatever makes my baby happy," Marsha's mother said, patting her daughter's hand. "When you look at these, which one makes you feel like a smile?"

Callie saw Regina bite her lip, and had to do the same. Some clients were difficult. Some were annoying. Some were easy as pie. And some…

Were Marshas.

Marsha stepped forward, picked up one glass, then the other. Studied it, put it down, sighed, then tried again. She glanced over at the Polaroids she'd had Regina take, so that she could get an idea of the way the table would look during the wedding, then glanced again at the glasses. "They both do. They both say pink to me."

"Well, which one would Samuel like?"

"Oh, the tall one, for sure. Because he likes things that are tall."

The logic swept right past Callie, but that might have been because her mind wasn't on the bride and her mother, but on Jared. On his research—

And his betrayal. How could he have done that to her?

She'd thought that he'd been a different man, the nice guy she'd known back in high school and college. And for a while there, she'd even thought maybe she was falling for him. Silly plan she'd had to make up for hurting him all those years ago.

Because all she'd done was go and hurt herself in the process.

"Callie? Are you listening?"

Marsha's voice drew her back to the ballroom. "Sorry, what'd you ask?"

"Weren't you listening?" Marsha pouted. "This is a critical decision."

"Oh, yes, it is," Callie said. "I, ah, was thinking about your floral design and how it would look with these glasses."

Regina sent her a thumbs-up and a mouthed, "Good save."

"Which one?" Marsha asked, her face full of panic. "Which one will be better with the flowers?"

Callie picked up the lean, tall glasses with the hearts. "These. They're closer in design to the types of flowers we're using, especially the lilies and the daisies. And, your dress has these same elegant, clean lines." Thanks to Serena and her deft hand at design.

Marsha beamed. "Oh, it does, doesn't it? Oh, yes, these. Definitely these." She let out a sigh. "I feel so much better now. Like the hardest decisions are made."

Marsha's mother patted her daughter's hand, her Pomeranian looking on with a decidedly jealous pout. "Yes, dear, they are. Except for the caterer. We still have that stressful choice between the tuna steaks and the salmon with puff pastry. Perhaps we should just go back to chicken."

Callie wanted to remind Marsha that the most important decisions about her future had nothing to do with puff pastry or stemware or vases, but all to do with the man she was choosing. Whether he would remember the way she took her eggs in the morning or forgot her birthday, or break her heart almost immediately after he put the ring on her finger because he found someone else, and then she'd end up spending the next nine years of her life trying to figure out how to put it back together, thinking it was something that she could fix—

And then realizing it hadn't been fixable after all.

Marsha and her mother finished up their decisions about the rest of the table settings, with Callie making a note for the hall about adding pink bows to the silverware, then the mother-daughter duo finally headed off to their appointment with the caterer. As they walked out the door, they started arguing about the merits of tuna versus salmon, which was more pink, thereby making the meal match the wedding better. Callie shook her head.

"So," Regina said, after the client was gone and Regina began gathering up her photography equipment, "what has you so distracted? Is it Jared?"

Callie let out a sigh. "Yes." She told Regina about what had happened after the Henry wedding, feeling better after she got the story off her chest. It helped, Callie realized, to share the heartache with someone who cared.

"Aw, Callie. Why didn't you tell anyone about this sooner?" Regina asked.

"There was Audra's wedding and all that she was going through. She needed the sympathy more than I did." Audra, though still upset by her fiancé's public betrayal, had rebounded pretty well and was back at work, happily up to her elbows in financial statements. For Audra, keeping busy kept her mind off of what had happened at her botched wedding.

"Callie, we're a team. We're here for each other, no matter what." Regina drew her into a quick hug. "Are you sure you're doing okay?"

Callie nodded. "Besides, he's not really my type."

"Is that something you're telling yourself or is it really true?" The two of them grabbed their coats, shrugged into them and started walking out of the ballroom, sending a wave toward the manager of the venue as they did. He gave them a weary goodbye, clearly glad the Schumacher ordeal was over, too.

"Both, I guess," Callie admitted. "Years ago, I didn't see Jared as the kind of guy I'd go for. Back then, he always had his head in a book. We were lab partners and study partners, but he never seemed like a guy you'd date, more the one you'd ask about your Bunsen burner."

Regina laughed. "I take it from the look on your face that despite everything that man has been making your Bunsen burner simmer."

Callie shrugged, then grinned. "Okay, yes, he does. And I hate that he does."

"Well, if you're smiling, he can't be all bad, can he?"

"I don't know." Callie sighed. They'd reached the sidewalk, and Callie paused to draw in a burst of cool spring air. "He hurt me, Regina. He really

did. I wanted to trust him, to believe he was different from all the other guys and to think
maybe…"

"He was the one?" Regina finished.

Callie nodded. "I thought that about him once
before. Back in college, but then—"

"What?" Regina asked when Callie didn't
finish.

"Tony came roaring back into my life. Tony
always seemed so exciting. So daring. Ready to
take on the world and ride off into the sunset, with
me on the back of his motorcycle." Callie drew in
a breath, then let it go. "That's what I was looking
for. Someone who would take me away from everything I hated. That was Tony, at least to me. Mr.
Excitement."

"What happened?"

"Mr. Excitement got bored with me and went
looking for other women." Callie shook her head,
then unlocked her Toyota and waited while Regina
climbed inside the passenger's side. After Callie had
the car started and had pulled away from the curb,
she started talking again. "I wasn't enough. And
with Jared, it turns out I'm just a research project."

The betrayal stung again, and Callie blinked
rapidly, clearing her vision. How could Jared, of
all people, have done that?

"Callie, I saw the way that man looked at you at

the Henry wedding, and there is no way he's thinking facts and figures when you're with him. Trust me, if Dell looked at me the way Jared looks at you, we'd have the entire Boston Fire Department hosing down the house every single night." Regina laid a hand over Callie's. "Jared may have started out thinking only of his Bunsen burners, but believe me, he's not anymore."

"Maybe. But that isn't what's been worrying me." Callie slowed for a red light, then drummed her fingers on the steering wheel and turned to face Regina. "What if I fall in love?"

"What's so bad about that?"

"I've been down that road before, Regina, and it didn't work out so well."

"That doesn't mean the second time can't go much better."

"That doesn't mean the second time is guaranteed to work out better, though."

"True." Regina glanced away from Callie, watching out the window as a light rain began to fall, misting on the windows, then drizzling down the glass in a zigzag of skinny droplets. "There aren't always guarantees when it comes to love or marriages."

The way Regina said it, Callie got the feeling her friend was talking about more than just Callie's life. "How are things going with Dell?"

"We're okay. We didn't get off to the best of starts, given how fast we got married. But we'll be all right. We just need time together." Regina turned back to Callie. "Anyway, back to you. What's your plan from here?"

Callie gave Regina a lopsided grin. "Run away."

"That's no way to deal with a problem."

"That's the only way I know." Callie had said the words as a joke, but she hadn't meant them that way. Still, she couldn't bring herself to tell any of the Belles her true thoughts about leaving. She knew it would hurt them, and the last thing she wanted to do was that. These women were her friends, and finding a way to explain her need to escape had become an almost insurmountable task. In a few days, she would, Callie decided. She'd have to.

This staying in one place thing clearly wasn't what Callie was meant for. She couldn't go on with her job, helping to put on weddings, designing the flowers, throwing the rice, wishing people well, when she didn't even believe in the concept of happily ever after.

It was time to move on. Trouble was, she couldn't seem to put one foot in front of the other.

Jared took Pope's advice. At least, part of it.

He went to Downtown Crossing, but stopped in

at three different places before he found what he was looking for. The salesperson gave him a dubious look, but Jared plunked down his credit card and insisted on the purchase.

Then he went to find the only person he knew who could talk Callie into something as insane as this.

Belle.

There'd be no escape, at least not today.

After Callie dropped Regina off at the Wedding Belles office, she headed home, wanting only to curl up on her couch with a good book, a glass of wine and a little solitude.

But when she pulled in front of her apartment building, she noticed a rental car parked in the space for her unit. Callie groaned, then headed inside.

"Callie!" Her mother exploded forward when Callie rounded the corner. "You're home!"

Callie was immediately enveloped in an Elizabeth Arden-scented hug. "Mom. I thought you were staying on the beach in Bermuda with your friend."

Her mother waved a hand, jeweled rings on her fingers and bracelets dangling from her wrists, all gifts from past husbands and boyfriends. "It didn't work out. He was only interested in me for my tan lines, if you know what I mean. So I hopped on a plane and here I am. Anyway, I couldn't wait to see you and catch up. I want to hear all about what's going on in your life. How work is, who you're dating." Her mother grinned. "If he has any friends."

"Mom, you just got divorced, what last week?"

"Exactly. Which means there's an opening in my heart." She pressed a hand to her chest and grinned, then tipped her head to the side, causing her light brown pageboy to swing. "So, do you want to go out? Go get some dinner?"

"I'm wiped out from the day. Let's order takeout."

Her mother pouted, disappointment shining in her green eyes. "I'd really rather go out. You know how I hate to stay home."

Callie did. Her mother never had been one for being a homebody. She liked to be out, be seen, to meet people, especially the next man to fill the vacancy, as she liked to put it.

And all Callie had ever wanted was a mother who would sit around the kitchen table, share a cup of tea and talk with her about her day—and listen, really listen. But she didn't say any of that. There wouldn't be any point.

Instead she told her mother to give her a minute to change, and agreed to go back into the city again for dinner.

They ended up in a crowded, noisy seafood place that Callie's mother had seen reviewed as *the* hotspot to visit in Boston. "It was at the top of the list in the airline magazine," Vanessa said. "I'm sure we'll meet lots of interesting people there."

"Mom, I don't need to meet interesting people. I'd really rather just visit with you."

"We can do that anytime." She glanced around the crowded bar. "Do you think we'll see any celebrities? Are they filming any movies in Boston right now?"

Callie sighed. "I don't know." They sat down for dinner, ordered two seafood meals that sounded delicious, then sat across from each other and had a people-watching conversation.

"Oh, look over there," Vanessa said, scanning the room. "Isn't that…? No. It couldn't be."

Callie turned and followed the direction her mother indicated and saw—

Jared Townsend, and his ubiquitous clipboard. Of all the restaurants in a city this large, he had to be here? Doing his research?

Was he following her? Callie felt a rush of regret for agreeing to her mother's idea about going out, wishing for the thirtieth time that she had opted to stay home.

But then she looked again and her heart constricted, the part of her that still cared about him, still reacted when she saw him in a suit and tie. Damned hormones. When would she stop reacting to that man? Stop caring about him?

All the more reason to leave town, to get away.

"Is that him?" her mother asked.

"Yes," Callie said, turning back around.

Her mother arched a brow. "You don't sound very surprised. I take it you knew he was in town?"

Callie shrugged, trying to act noncommittal, unconcerned. "I've seen him around."

"Well then, let's call him over. Have a little reunion of sorts. Go ahead, Callie. Invite him to join us." But before Callie could even refuse, her mother rose. "Jared! Jared!"

"Mom," Callie whispered, acutely aware that people were staring. "He's working. Leave him alone."

"How can he be working in a restaurant?" Her mother sucked in a breath, then gaped at Callie. "Oh Lord. He's not a busboy, is he? Oh, and I thought he would go so far. He seemed so smart."

"He's a research scientist. He's working on a survey."

"In a *restaurant?* Is he working for those fast food people?" Her mother finally caught Jared's attention and sat back down. "Oh, good. He's coming over."

Oh, no. Callie did not want to see him. She and

Jared were over, let it stay that way. She'd managed to avoid his phone calls, his cards, his flowers, every attempt he'd made to contact her. The last thing she needed was her mother forcing some kind of matchmaking attempt. "Mom, really, let him do his job."

"Why, Calandra January Phillips, if I didn't know better, I'd think you didn't want him to sit with us."

Callie cringed at the use of her full name, which her mother had chosen because it meant "lark," her favorite bird, and the middle name, to remind her of the month of her birth. As soon as Callie could talk, she'd started insisting on her nickname. "Mom, *please*. Can't you and I just visit? For once?"

Her mother gave her a blank look. "What do we have to talk about? I've known you all your life. You'd think we'd have said everything by now."

"Yeah, of course we have." Callie shook her head and muttered a quick prayer that her mother wouldn't launch into another one of her Top Ten Reasons Why This Man Should Marry My Daughter speeches.

As long as Vanessa didn't whip out any visual aids, Callie figured she'd be safe.

"Mrs. Phillips," Jared said, arriving at their table. "It's nice to see you again."

"Actually, I'm not Mrs. Phillips anymore, or

Mrs. Linden, or Mrs. Spires, or any of the other names. I'm officially on the market again, if you know any older men." She laughed, then waved at the empty chair beside her. "Sit down, Jared. There's no reason for a man like you to eat alone, especially on a Friday night."

Jared looked to Callie. She tried to send him a mental no, but all he did was grin and pull out the chair. What was he thinking? Hadn't she made it clear she wanted nothing to do with him?

"Why thank you," Jared said. "I don't mind if I do."

"Now tell me, what's with that clipboard?" Vanessa asked. "Callie says it's some kind of research. What exactly are you doing?"

Jared's gaze met Callie's, a burst of heat exchanged in that look—hers in anger, his with something else—before he returned his attention to her mother. "I'm studying relationships and love. Whether real people fall in love at first sight, how true love develops and what makes people who love each other stay together."

Her mother leaned forward, her attention rapt on Jared. "And what'd you find out so far?"

"That sometimes people aren't as honest as they think, at least when it comes to love."

Callie resisted the urge to blurt out a sarcastic retort.

"Isn't that the truth," Vanessa said. "I've been down that aisle four times and not one of my husbands has been honest. I must have liar radar or something, because I just can't pick them very well."

"Maybe you need to quit picking them," Jared said. "If you don't mind me saying so."

Her mother cocked her head and studied him. "What do you mean, stop picking them?"

"Well, my research has shown that the relationships that last work much better when the man has pursued the woman, proving that old axiom about boy chases girl. When the woman makes the choice and makes it a little too…easy on the man, he seems to lose interest and move on, maybe something to do with the hunter instinct, I think. If you make a man work for what he wants, he tends to, ah, toe the line a little better." Jared gestured toward Callie's mother. "Not that I'm implying that you have done anything of the sort, of course."

"Oh, but I have, I have. I'm a total chaser. Like a dog after a Honda, that's me. Except when it came to my first husband, who took off over and over again and I just gave up going after him. Clearly some dogs don't want to stay leashed." Her mother took a sip of wine, then shook her head. "Wow. That's an entirely new way of looking at dating. Sort of *Field of Dreams* for dating."

"*Field of Dreams?*" Jared asked.

Vanessa grinned and then waved a hand over her voluptuous figure. "If you build it, they will come calling." She patted Jared's hand, then rose. "Thank you for that bit of advice, Jared. Now, I'm going to go powder my nose and leave you two alone for a bit. Maybe someone at this table has a little unfinished business to pursue, too. Hmm?"

Callie watched her mother leave, then turned back to Jared. What was all that he'd been talking about with his research? She'd seen nothing of the sort in his notebook. She shrugged it off, and decided to try to convince him to leave while she still had a chance—and before she got distracted by the way he filled out his suit, or the memory of his kiss. Both of which were still imprinted on her mind, seeming to override her better sense, like congressmen vetoing a budget bill. "You don't have to stay, Jared. I can make up an excuse when my mother comes back. I'll tell her that you had to go back to work or something."

Jared grinned. "Oh, but I do want to stay, Callie."

"Even if you're not welcome?"

"I was invited over. Remember?"

"By my mother, not me."

He leaned forward, and when he did, Callie inhaled the scent of his cologne, a mix of woods and man, and everything within her fought against being mad at him. The vetoes were going up fast and furious.

"What's it going to take for you to forgive me?" he said.

"I can't, Jared. I—" She shook her head, refusing to be dissuaded by the grin on his lips, the way she could fall into his eyes. "Let me put it in terms you'd understand. I fed in the numbers for you and me, added the numbers and our two and two came out to five."

"Callie—"

"No, Jared. We don't belong together. We're not even close to the same kind of people. You're a traditionalist and I'm not. In fact, I'm not even staying here."

His eyes widened. "What do you mean?"

"I mean, I'm leaving again," she said, the decision made now. As long as Jared would be nearby, and the possibility of running into him—and falling for him—still existed, she couldn't stay. "I'm going to give my notice to Belle and move on. I can't keep putting on a happy face at all these weddings when I don't even believe in getting married."

He shook his head and sat back. "I never thought I'd see the day."

"What are you talking about?"

Then he pitched toward her again and leaned in close, very close, so close he could have kissed her with nothing more than a breeze to bring them together. "I never thought I'd see the day when Callie Phillips chickened out."

Jared got to his feet, grabbed his clipboard and left her there. Openmouthed, and at a total loss for words.

CHAPTER ELEVEN

CALLIE clicked on screen after screen on her computer. Dozens of options, taking her everywhere from Maine to Monte Carlo.

And not a single one appealed to her.

Instead of the usual rush of anticipation she had always felt before, another emotion clutched at her throat, twisted in her gut.

Loss.

But she saw no other way out. How could she possibly stay here, working all day on weddings? How could she put her heart into creating other women's wedding dreams when that heart no longer believed in those dreams?

"That doesn't look like a floral research trip to me, darlin'." Belle's voice, soft and concerned, came from over Callie's shoulder.

She froze, a lump thick in her throat. Callie minimized the screens, then turned in her chair. "Belle. I didn't know you were there."

"Whatcha doin', honey?"

Callie drew in a breath, then got honest. "Panicking."

Belle's laughter was full of understanding. "I've been there, just before I walked down the aisle the first time, the second time. The third time, too, come to think of it. But your case is a little worse than a touch of cold feet, isn't it?"

Callie nodded. "I've never been one for staying put."

"You've been here for three years."

"I know. That's the longest time I've spent anywhere," Callie said. "Maybe it's time I moved on. Did something else with my life."

Belle pulled up another chair and settled into it. "This doesn't have anything to do with that man you've been dating, does it? Has the professor got your dander all fluffed?"

Callie chuckled. "Dander all fluffed?"

"He's the one who's got you runnin' scared, isn't he?"

"I'm just so scared about all those what-ifs."

"What if what?" Belle said. "What if the earth starts turnin' in the other direction? What if dogs start dancing in the streets?" Belle threw up her hands. "Callie, you can't live your life waitin' on what might happen. You just grab hold and enjoy the ride."

Callie thought of the Tilt-A-Whirl, of how

she'd told Jared nearly the exact same thing. But falling for him was a much bigger step than getting on some carnival ride and spinning in a circle for three minutes.

"But there's more, isn't there?" Belle said softly.

There wasn't any sense in hiding the truth from Belle. Heck, from hiding it from herself. Jared, had indeed, been the one who had triggered the old instincts to flee. And if Callie planned to leave, she needed to tell Belle first. It was only fair. "Yes. It's more than Jared, it's something I've done all my life. Why do I do that? Why do I want to run every time a man gets close to me?"

"Well, darlin', if I knew the answer to that, I'd be marryin' again myself." Belle laughed. "I'm trying to stay clear of the aisle, too, but it seems like every man I meet wants either a wife or a maid. Maybe we should book double passage to wherever you're going." She gave Callie a wink.

"Oh, you'd never leave this place. The business. It's your heart and soul."

"No, I wouldn't." Belle's clear blue gaze met Callie's. "And neither should you. You fit here, Callie."

Callie looked around the room, at the elegant setting that somehow managed to feel comfortable, too. Maybe it was the yellow walls or the delicate pattern of the carpet. Maybe it was the spring flowers blooming outside the windows or the portraits of beaming brides and grooms on the walls.

No. Callie suspected what had really made her fit here over the past three years wasn't any of the furnishings or the details. It was Belle, and the women who made up the Belles. They had given her a home, not in a physical sense, but in her heart.

Belle laid a hand over Callie's. "Every time a squirrel runs from what scares him, he gets hit by a truck."

Callie laughed. "That's supposed to make me feel better?"

"No, it's supposed to make you laugh, and it did." Belle rose. "But it's also supposed to make you think. What's out there—" at that, Belle waved toward the windows, to the world beyond the shop "—isn't necessarily better than what is in here. You need to face what's scarin' you, darlin', before you can move on."

"But what if I don't know what I'm so scared of? What if I'm not sure why I want to run?"

"All the more reason to stay where you are, I say. Can't find the answers if you're always running from the questions." Belle gave her a smile that was filled with the wisdom of a woman who had traveled many of life's paths already, then left Callie to figure out the rest.

* * *

At the end of the day, Callie was the only one left in the shop. She'd worked extra late, burying herself in sketches, then the tedious task of sorting the mountain of silk flowers, a collection that often got jumbled during the busy season. Somehow, color-coding and cataloging the faux florals kept Callie's mind off Jared and his ridiculous notion that she was chickening out by leaving town.

The bell over the door rang and Callie dropped the bunch of flowers in her arms to the table and headed out to the reception area. A tall, older man with salt-and-pepper hair stood in the middle of the room, looking as lost as a Great Dane at a cat show. "Can I help you?" Callie asked.

"Uh…" The man glanced around, taking in the feminine surroundings, the bridal portraits, the pile of lacy blue garters lying on the table that had arrived by delivery a little while ago and Callie had forgotten to put away. He shuffled from foot to foot, then glanced up at her, as if he expected her to teleport him anywhere but there. "This isn't the kind of place I frequent."

"Most men don't, at least not until a woman drags them in here." Callie laughed.

The man echoed her laughter, then put out his hand. "Name's Charlie Wiley." He had a firm grip, and a friendly smile. "I'm, ah, looking for a woman named Belle."

"She's not here. Everyone's gone home for the day. But Belle lives upstairs and should be back in a half hour or so. She just left for some dinner." Callie gestured toward the settee. "You're welcome to wait."

Just then Marsha Schumacher came running through the door, in a flurry of pink, her polka-dotted dress topped by a pink trench coat to keep her dry from the drizzle outside. "Callie! You have to help me! I'm having a total marital meltdown. I need someone to talk to and Mother's at the spa having her eyes BOTOXed and her lips re-plumped. She won't be able to talk for at least an hour, and even then, I don't think she'll be able to properly emote." Marsha grabbed Callie's arm, as if she were about to hold her hostage. "I need you. This is an *emergency*."

Callie worked a smile to her face. She didn't know what advice she could give Marsha, but com-forting the brides was, after all, part of her job for as long as she worked at Wedding Belles. "Sure, Marsha."

"Oh, and there's a man here, too!" Marsha squealed, spying Charlie. "I could get your advice, too. On the whole guy perspective."

Charlie backed up, his discomfort clearly multiplying by the second. "That's, ah, not my area. I'll come back to talk to Belle. Later." He glanced again at Marsha. "Much later."

"Do you want me to give Belle a message?" Callie asked.

But Charlie had already headed out the door, hightailing it as fast as a man could. Callie would be willing to bet dollars to doughnuts that the man was one seriously confirmed bachelor.

"Oh, Callie," Marsha cried, grabbing Callie's hand and dragging her onto the settee, "he's backing out of the wedding!"

"Samuel? Why?"

"He thinks we need more time. That this is too big of a step to take so fast. Like being engaged for three months isn't long enough." Marsha raised tear-filled eyes to Callie's. "Don't you think he should know, in three months, if he loves me or not?"

"Well, Marsha, I don't know if I'm the best one to give you advice—"

"But you're a wedding planner. This is your job. You...you *have* to know." Marsha stared at her, expecting some wisdom to come tumbling from Callie's mouth, some answer to all the engagement questions in the cosmos.

"Well..." Callie paused, stalling, searching for something to say to Marsha. What was she supposed to say?

And then, the answer came to her, or at least, *an* answer.

"Maybe you've been concentrating on the wrong things, Marsha, and Samuel, well, he's been feeling left out."

"Concentrating on the wrong things?" Marsha cocked her head, her dark brown up-do falling a bit as she did. "Like the wedding? But that's the most important thing."

"Actually the marriage is. The relationship. The details, they don't really matter. The wedding is only a single day out of your life. The marriage is for the *rest* of your life."

"Well, that's a weird thing for you to say." Marsha frowned. "Isn't it your job to watch the details?"

"Exactly. That's *my* job, mine and the rest of the Belles," Callie said. "So that you can worry about the rest. You and Samuel."

Marsha sat back against the settee, her mouth opening, then closing. For the first time since Callie had met the outspoken bride, Marsha was at a loss for words. A good five seconds passed before the girl in pink said a thing. "No one really cares about the salmon with puff pastry, do they?"

"Well, maybe only the people who like tuna steaks." Callie grinned. "In the long run, Marsha, none of it matters. You could get married in your

backyard and serve peanut butter and jelly sandwiches, or get married in a million dollar
ceremony and hand out diamonds for favors, and
it won't make a difference in how happy you are
ten years down the road, if you're getting married
for all the wrong reasons."

Marsha smoothed a hand over her dress, then
glanced up at Callie, tears again shimmering in her
eyes. "How do I know what the right reasons are?"

"That's easy." Callie smiled. "Your heart will
tell you. What's your heart telling you?"

Marsha thought for a minute. "That I love
Samuel. And that I don't care about salmon with
puff pastry or tuna. Just marrying him."

"I think you answered your own question."

"Thank you," Marsha said. She swiped the tears
off her face. "You made me feel a lot better. I'm
going to call Samuel and straighten this all out.
And from here on out, I'll let the wedding
planners plan the wedding and Samuel and I, we'll
plan the marriage." Marsha surged forward and
gave Callie a tight, nearly suffocating hug, then
drew back. "You've been so great, Callie. You
must have a lot of experience with this kind of
thing, huh?"

"Not exactly. I was one of those people who
didn't listen to my heart until it was too late."

"You mean you let a good man get away?"

"Well, I—" Callie cut off the sentence. Had she done that?

She'd been about to tell Marsha about her divorce, but realized that when she thought about her heart, and what it was telling her about who'd gotten away, the first man who came to mind wasn't her ex-husband.

It was Jared.

The only trouble was reading the message.

Jared closed his high school yearbook, the mixed emotions churning in his gut. That period of his life had been immeasurably difficult as he'd tried to hold his family together even as it fractured beneath him.

Then he left his apartment and drove to the cemetery in Brookline. There, he found the graves of his parents. Two people who'd barely been able to live together in life, but who now lay side by side in death.

He bent down beneath his mother's stone, inserting fresh flowers into the vase. "I'm sorry," he whispered.

No one answered him back, of course. She'd been gone a year, his father more than fifteen years. Jared stayed there a long time, wondering if there was anything he could have done differently, knowing as always there really hadn't been, but wishing all the same.

Then he rose. It was well past time to stop living under that shadow.

And there was only one woman he wanted to take with him on his journey forward. Callie Phillips.

"I didn't know you could make puff pastry pink," Audra whispered to Callie when they arrived at the Schumacher wedding the next afternoon.

"Apparently anything can be made pink if you pay for it," Callie said, taking in the pink-silk draped walls, the pink bridesmaids, even the pink tuxedoed band. The silverware had, as promised, been bedecked with tiny pink bows. "But overall, it's not too bad, and I'm glad Marsha and Samuel worked everything out."

"Thanks to you, I hear." Audra gave Callie a curious look. "Since when did you become a card-carrying promarriage cheerleader?"

Callie grinned, as if this was nothing unusual. "Just doing my job."

"Uh-huh," Audra said, with a knowing smile. "Sounds like more than doing your job, but I'm not going to argue with you. Though, I am starting to buy into your theory about there not being enough Mr. Rights. Especially since my Mr. Right turned out to be Mr. Totally Wrong."

"I'm sorry about that, Audra. I really am."

Sympathy shimmered through Callie. How she would have rather seen Audra celebrating a happy ending, rather than herself. "I wish it had worked out for you."

"I'm okay with it. Better to know now than ten years down the road." Then Audra smiled, and Callie knew, as she had known the day of the botched wedding, that Audra would be okay. "And to know before our next poker game."

"Seriously, Audra, don't give up. There's still a perfect ending in store for you. I'm sure of it."

Audra stared at Callie. "You've changed."

"Me? No, not at all." Then she let out a nervous laugh, as Audra continued her suspicious perusal. "I'm just trying to win a bet."

Audra dug in her purse and pulled out a quarter, placing it in Callie's palm. The metal was cold, oddly heavy for such a small piece. "You did win, didn't you?"

It had started out as a joke, and now, Callie regretted ever agreeing to the silly bet. How weird was that?

She stared at the silver coin, an ordinary quarter. She should have been happy. She had, after all, won. This was what she'd wanted. To prove, once and for all, that putting stock in such a ridiculous notion as a perfect man for every woman was crazy.

She'd won.

But won what?

The proof that she would end up unhappy and alone? If that was the prize, Callie didn't want it. She turned the quarter over in her palm, heads, tails, heads, tails.

Neither side seemed to offer a win.

She went to pocket the coin, then changed her mind and dropped it back into Audra's hand. "No. I can't take it."

Audra's brows arched. "Why?"

"This sounds crazy, but for some reason, I just can't give up that last little bit of hope." She gestured toward Marsha and Samuel, dancing cheek to cheek, appearing now like the world's happiest couple. A rumbling of envy tightened in Callie's gut. How she wanted that for herself, even in its pink-wrapped bubble. "Call me sentimental, but I guess I still want to think that maybe…"

"Maybe it's possible. For you," Audra drew in a breath, "and me?"

Callie nodded, meeting Audra's gaze with a shared connection of understanding. "Maybe. Just maybe."

"I understand," Audra said softly.

For a long time, they just watched the happy couple, two friends who didn't need to say a word to know what the other was thinking.

Then Callie spotted her mother across the room, chatting up an older man. Scoping out husband number five? Already? "Or maybe not. Excuse me, Audra. I have someone else I need to talk to."

She rose and crossed the room, reaching her mother just as Vanessa was accepting a glass of wine from the older, distinguished looking gentleman. "Mom. Want to get some air?"

"Sure. Have you met Samuel's father?"

"The groom's father?" Oh, this went too far. Callie opened her mouth to protest, ready to haul her mother out of there when Vanessa waved over the man's wife and completed the introductions.

"I was just telling them what a wonderful thing you did yesterday when you talked to Marsha and calmed her right down," Callie's mother said. "It was just so sweet of Marsha to invite me to the wedding, too. Now there's a girl who knows the importance of mothers."

Callie blinked in surprise. She'd thought her mother was flirting with Samuel's father when in fact she'd actually been singing her daughter's praises? That was a change of pace Callie hadn't expected. The band announced the beginning of the *hora*, so Samuel's parents said their goodbyes and made their way over to participate in the event.

"Let's go outside, Mom," Callie said. A pair of French doors beside the bar led to a private outdoor patio, which Callie had decorated earlier with swooping garlands of stargazer lilies, Gerbera daisies and ivy, matching the table arrangements. The afternoon sun had released the heady perfume of the flowers, giving the air a sweet scent. Callie paused, drawing in the fragrance of her work. "I love flowers. Something about them just makes me…happy."

"Then why are you thinking about quitting your job?"

She turned toward her mother. "How did you know that?"

"I didn't spend all those years with your father and not learn a thing or two about learning to read the signals, Callie." Vanessa took a seat at one of the wrought-iron tables, then waited while her daughter sat in the opposite chair.

"To be honest, I didn't think you paid all that much attention to what I was doing."

Her mother sipped at her wine, watching the sun for a long moment, as the golden orb started its descent toward the horizon. "I haven't been so good at that, have I?"

"No."

"Maybe if I had been…" Vanessa shook her head. "Well, if I'd concentrated more on what had been going on at home, maybe your father might have been more interested in hanging around." Her eyes met her daughter's, and in that moment of connection, Callie realized they had each lost something every time Joseph Phillips had walked out.

"Do you think we shut him out? Weren't there for him?"

"Callie, we stayed. We kept trying." Vanessa snorted. "I don't know why. He was the one who left us. Over and over again."

Callie fingered one of the delicate stargazer lilies, running a fingertip along the deep pink valley of the blossom. "Do you know why I love stargazer lilies? Because they don't conform. They're one of the most fragrant flowers available and that drives growers crazy."

If her mother found the turn in conversation odd, she didn't say anything. Instead she rose, crossed to the flowers and bent to inhale the scent of the lily. "They're heavenly. Why don't growers like them?"

"The more scent a flower has, the more energy it uses up producing the fragrance. Scent, though, is only good for pollinating. There's no need for that in commercial growing, and when a flower like this lily has used up most of its energy to smell pretty, that means its beauty won't last as long."

"So it's not as profitable."

Callie nodded. "It's a square peg in all those round holes. But to me, it's perfect. Bold and dramatic, and so beautiful."

Vanessa cupped a bloom in her palm, studying the delicately dotted petals. "They are beautiful. And what you do with them, honey, is amazing."

"Thank you," Callie said, a smile curving across her face. Her mother had noticed her work, maybe for the first time ever. Joy soared in her heart. Such a silly thing, really, especially at her age, but she supposed a child never really grew too old for a mother's praise.

"You know," Vanessa said, returning to the table, retrieving her wine, "I've been thinking a lot about what Jared said the other night. About chasing after men. And I realized I've been chasing after things all my life. Running, like you."

"Like Dad."

Silence extended between them, as the truth sank in between mother and daughter. "That is what we did, isn't it?"

"It was a lot easier than trying to figure out why he kept leaving us, wasn't it?" Tears filled Callie's eyes, tears for unanswered questions, ones that might never be answered, because the man who held the answers never sat still long enough to tell either of them what they so desperately wanted to know.

A single tear ran down her mother's face, then another, belying all of Vanessa's bravado. She, too, had been hurt by Joseph's continual departures.

"Why did he do it, Mom? Weren't we good enough?" Callie's voice broke, the last syllables shredded in the question she'd never spoken aloud before.

It was the one question she'd never asked her father. Never asked her first husband.

Hadn't she been good enough? Good enough to stay home for? Good enough for forever?

Good enough to love?

Vanessa reached forward then, gathering Callie into her arms. "Of course you were, baby, of course you were. We both were, even if we didn't think so." She wrapped her comfort around her daughter, soothing and saying everything that Callie had needed to hear, but still, she wondered, still, she needed to know.

"Why?" Callie asked. "Why did he keep leaving?"

"I don't know. I asked him, Callie, every time, and he just said that staying around wasn't for him."

The words blasted Callie like ice water. How many times had she said that herself? To landlords, bosses, Tony?

Jared?

Had she turned into the very person she didn't want to be? The one who'd abandoned her over and over again? And all under the guise of wanting to have fun, take risks, live life by her own rules?

"I've looked for Dad, everywhere I've gone," Callie said after a while, the words taking their time to make their journey from her heart to her lips. "And I even found him once, in Mexico City. He seemed so glad to see me, and said he wanted to get to know me, spend time with me again." She remembered how hope had fluttered in her heart like a butterfly, so fragile and new, how she'd gone home to the apartment she and Tony had been renting, bursting with joy that this time, this time would be different with her father.

But Tony hadn't been there to tell. He'd been out with someone else, as usual. And when she'd gone that night, hurrying so she wouldn't be late, carrying pictures of her trips, a pile of letters that had been sent and returned to sender, and most of all, hope in her heart for a connection that had always been as fragile as dried baby's breath, to meet with her father again—

He'd been gone.

"But he didn't stay, Mom. He left." Callie's voice broke, and she hung her head.

Her mother's arms went around her again, drawing her daughter in, the years of distance melting in that moment, of one woman telling another she understood her pain, and wanted so badly to take it away. "I think he was afraid. Afraid that he couldn't close the gap anymore." She tipped Callie's face up to meet hers. "I've done the same thing, Callie. I'm so sorry."

"We both did." Tears slipped out of Callie's eyes, marring her makeup, but she didn't care. She let them come. They were too far overdue. "I'm sorry, too."

"*Is* it too late?" Vanessa asked, her gaze watery, her voice shaky. Her hold on her daughter tight, yet tenuous. "Too late to close the gap? With you? And me?"

Callie couldn't answer her. The words lodged in her throat, stuck behind the lump. Instead she shook her head, whispered no, then wrapped her arms tight around her mother.

And didn't let go for a long, long time.

"Darlin', you are either completely crazy or totally in love," Belle said. She shook her head, laughed again, then waved Jared on in. "If Callie finds out I had anything to do with this, she's bound to start telling people my real age."

Jared chuckled and put up his right hand. "I'll keep your name out of it. Scout's honor. Do you have what I needed?"

Belle nodded then turned and reached into her bag and handed the small black object to Jared. "You're definitely crazy, darlin', but the kind of crazy I like. You'll find Callie outside, on the patio. You go get her and I'll set everything else up." Belle caught his arm before he walked away. "You're sure you can get her to do this? She's one determined filly."

"Well, I'm not planning on taking no for an answer." He gave Belle a grin, then headed across the room. He didn't see the bride, the groom, the crowd of guests, any of the busy reception. He had one destination in mind, and one person.

He found her, as Belle had said, on the patio, with her mother, the two of them talking about the flowers draping the wrought-iron fence. When he stepped through the doors, the two women stopped midsentence and pivoted toward him. "Jared," Callie said, surprise rising the pitch in her voice. "What are you doing here?"

"Looking for you." He had to take a breath, as his gaze swept over her and the impact of seeing her again slammed into him. She was dressed in a simple cranberry-colored dress with a scoop neck, leaving her arms bare, outlining her waist, her hips. The skirt swung around her legs, allowing him a delicious peek at the curve of her calves, enhanced by a pair of high heels with tiny rhinestones marching across the ankle. She'd swept her hair up and tucked it back with little sparkly combs, exposing the graceful swoop of her neck.

But it was her lips—always her lips and the crimson lipstick—that drew his attention again and again. He wanted to draw her to him, feel her in his arms again, and kiss her until everything that stood between them had melted away.

But even Jared knew it wouldn't be that simple. If it were, then the last few times he'd done that would have solved everything.

"I'll leave you two alone," Vanessa said, giving them a smile before slipping back in to join the wedding. As she passed him, she gave Jared a pat on the shoulder.

"We settled all this earlier, Jared," Callie said. "I don't have anything to say to you."

He grinned. "I expected that argument. And I came armed with a rebuttal."

"A rebuttal?"

"Yep." He took a step closer, the fragrance of the lilies and daisies wrapping around her, as if the flowers she worked with were a part of her. Jared trailed a finger along the neckline of her dress, watching as her eyes widened, her breath quickened, and knew that no matter what Callie said, nothing was settled between them. Not by a long shot. "I'm not here to argue with you, to dance with you or to kiss you, as much as I want to do that."

She didn't answer and a part of him wondered if she was thinking about kissing him, too.

"I'm here to make sure that you take a walk on the wild side tonight. Well, maybe not the wild side, but a definite walk into unfamiliar territory."

"What are you talking about?"

He reached into the breast pocket of his suit and pulled out the item Belle had given him earlier and placed it in Callie's palm. "Get up on that stage, Miss Callie Phillips, and sing."

She stared at the microphone in her hand as if it might bite her. "Sing? Are you crazy? Why would I do that?"

"Because all you ever do is run away, Callie. You're planning on doing it again, you told me so yourself." She looked away and he could tell she hadn't changed her mind. Disappointment slammed into him, but he pressed on. "You can go ahead and leave, but before you do, I want you to do one thing. Tonight I want you to stay and actually *tackle* your dreams instead of leaving them behind."

"I don't—"

He put a finger over her lips, tension coiling in

his body, the need to kiss her so real and tangible, Jared felt like he could pluck it out of the air. "I know you do, because I've been doing it myself, too, all my life. And I'm tired of it. In fact, today, when I turned in my research project, I quit my job."

"You did what?"

"I gave my two weeks' notice. And I applied to work at one of those think tanks. But in a way, I kind of hope I don't get the job."

She gaped at him as if he'd grown three heads and a unicorn horn. "You, Mr. Dependable, actually want to be unemployed?"

He grinned. "Yeah. A wise man I know told me it's fun to skate on the edge of life. I think I might try it. At least until the rent's due."

Callie laughed. "So you're skating, but wearing a helmet?"

"Exactly." He chuckled, then sobered. "Tonight, though, isn't about me, it's about you. Go on out on the stage and show everyone what you can do."

Callie shook her head, trying to hand back the mike, but Jared wouldn't take it. "I can't do that. Belle would never—"

He cut off her objections by spinning her toward the reception and pointing at the stage. "You can. I already talked to the band and Marsha and

Samuel know all about it, too. Everything is all set up. The only missing ingredient is you."

"You set this up?" She veered back at him. "How did you know I'd even say yes?"

"I didn't." Jared shrugged. "But I wasn't going to leave here until you did. And if worse came to worst, I'd have gotten up there and sung until you came to put me out of my misery."

"Why? Why would you do this for me, Jared?"

"Because—" But before he could get the words out, the leader of the band announced Callie's guest appearance and the wedding guests swiveled their attention toward Callie, erupting into applause. Her friends rushed over, calling her name, waving her on. And Callie was gone, heading toward the stage, the microphone in her hands, and her dream underway.

Jared stayed long enough to watch Callie sing her first song. He stayed at the back of the room, allowing the notes of the song, the sweet melody of Callie's voice, to wash over him, treasuring every note that slipped from her lips. At first, she stood stiff and nervous, but with each stanza, Callie relaxed, falling into a rhythm with the band.

She was a natural performer, just as Jared had known she'd be. He stayed until she reached the last notes of the chorus, then he headed for the exit.

"Jared," Vanessa called, catching up to him. "Where are you going?"

"I did what I came to do," he said, taking one last look at Callie and hoping like hell it wouldn't be the very last one. "The rest is up to her."

CHAPTER TWELVE

"How'd it go last night, man?" Pope asked when Jared returned to the office.

"It didn't." Jared grabbed a small box off the shelf and began loading in the few personal possessions he'd kept on his desk over the years he'd worked at Wiley Games. A Caffeine Stimulates Deep Thinking coffee mug. A suspense novel he'd been meaning to read and never had. A Dilbert stress ball Pope had given him as a joke, probably because of the resemblance. And a picture of him and Callie, a decade old, that he'd tucked into the bulletin board when he'd first moved to Boston. He stared at the image for a long time, then slipped the photo between the pages of the novel.

"So you're just quitting?"

"Yep. As of yesterday, I'm finished." Jared looked over at Pope. "Oh, I'm not quitting on her. The job."

Pope sank into a chair. "Phew. Good thing. I was

getting worried about you, dude. Glad to see you got your priorities straight. Unemployment is way easier to take than a broken heart. I know, because—" Pope looked away.

Jared lowered the box to his desk. "You okay, bud?"

"Yeah. Me and my girl, we had a fight and she broke up with me." Pope heaved a sigh and Jared could swear he saw a tear in the eyes of the guy who also sported an earring.

"Well, maybe the, ah, Lethargio approach is not the best one. Perhaps you should step it up." Jared gestured to the report he'd compiled from the data. "According to my research, what women want is a man who keeps pursuing them, no matter what. Who won't give up, even when it seems as if all is lost. Sort of like passing a test…" His voice trailed off and he stared at the green folder holding all the answers. He should have hit himself with all the numbers he'd been compiling, instead of shoving them into the computer. "I'm a complete idiot."

Pope popped out of his chair. "No, dude, you're brilliant. That's exactly what I needed to hear. That's the perfect answer. I'm heading over there right now, to show her I'm a total warrior dude in love."

Pope ran out of the room, as full of fire as an ancient Scotsman on the battlefield. Pope may have been younger, but Jared was more motivated and he passed him easily in the hall.

Jared had some statistics to prove and this time, he didn't care one whit that his hypothesis was based completely on a personal theory.

And that the only possible outcome was marriage.

"Girls, we have a wedding to plan."

Belle stood in the middle of the reception area of the offices for the Wedding Belles, her face lit with a massive smile. She held a bottle of champagne in one hand, a half dozen champagne flutes in the other. "This one is going to put the Wedding Belles on the map. And then some."

Audra, Regina, Natalie, Julie, Serena and Callie gathered around Belle, the six of them pausing in their work, confusion on their faces. "What wedding are you talking about?" Audra asked.

"Does the name Liz Vandiver mean anything to you gals?" Belle beamed. "As in *the* Vandivers?"

"Oh my gosh!" Serena gasped, putting a hand to her chest. "You mean the really, really wealthy Vandivers? The ones that are always in the gossip columns?"

Belle nodded. "Yep. Apparently their daughter was a guest at one of our weddings and she wants the Wedding Belles to put her dream together. Us.

Can you believe it?" Belle laid the champagne flutes on the coffee table, then unwrapped the foil and popped the cork on the bottle of bubbly. The cork exploded off the top of bottle, pinging off the armchair. Champagne flowed in a stream of gold from the neck. "Whoops!" Belle laughed, then filled each of the glasses and dispensed them to the Belles. "This is a great thing for us. It's a huge wedding—a big bucks wedding at that—and we need to celebrate!"

The women cheered and toasted, laughter pouring out of them faster than the champagne. "Oh, what a great financial boon this will be," Audra said, clearly mentally calculating the profit margin. "And think of the word of mouth we'll get."

"When the pictures of the wedding get into the newspapers and magazines," Regina added, walking around the room, seeming to frame the images already in her mind, "it'll give us even more exposure. I can only imagine how much this will do for the Wedding Belles business."

Serena nodded. "It's great to see everything looking up for all of us, for a change."

Julie raised her glass. "Hear, hear. I'm all for an increase in business."

Callie had stayed silent, though she was glad for the news. She sipped at her champagne, smiling with her friends. But her mind was on Jared, on last night. After the Vandiver wedding news celebration had died down and the rest of the women had left for a group consultation with another bride and groom at the Marriott Hotel, Belle pulled her aside.

"You were awfully quiet, darlin'. Everything okay?"

Callie nodded, avoided Belle's inquisitive gaze by plucking dead leaves off one of the plants in the entry room. "Just tired. Late night last night."

"I'll say. How many songs did you sing with the band? A dozen?" Belle gave her a wide smile. "You have quite the talent, my girl."

"Thanks." Callie grinned. "I don't know why I was so afraid to show you. It was a lot of fun. And you, I hear, were in on the conspiracy."

"I'm not above a little conspirin', when it's in your best interests." Belle grinned. "Seems that Jared knew you better than you knew yourself. He told me that if I was smart, I'd add a part-time wedding singer to my operation." Belle cocked her head and studied Callie. "You interested in the job?"

Callie opened her mouth, closed it. "Well, I...I never really thought about doing that."

Belle laid her champagne flute on the table and began circling the perimeter of the room, straightening pillows, acting nonchalant. "You know, this Vandiver wedding will be a lot of work. It'll require all of us to pull together. I can't take this one on, if I'm going to be a woman short. Can I count on you to stay?"

Hidden meaning—was she still going to leave town?

Callie stood in the room that she had grown to love over the past three years and considered the woman who had become a second mother. She thought of the future that lay ahead of her here. A future filled with flowers, and with a little bit of singing, if she wanted it.

To have those things meant permanence. The very thing Callie had shied away from for so many years.

"If you're going to stay, you might even want to think about buying a little house," Belle said. "Maybe planting some of those flowers you love so much."

"A garden, huh?" Callie grinned. "Are you trying to convince me to put down roots?"

"Is it that obvious?"

Callie laughed. "Yes."

Belle returned to Callie's side, her touch gentle on Callie's arm. "It's not so bad, you know. Roots hold a person firm; give them something to stand on when a storm rolls in."

Callie thought about that. About all the times when she'd turned tail, instead of staying in one place when her life got hard, then thought of how much easier it had been to go through her divorce because she'd stayed here, stayed with her friends, her job.

Where would she want to be the next time a storm rolled in? Some distant land? A foreign city? A strange town? Alone?

Or right here, surrounded by the people who loved her, the things she loved?

"Stargazer lilies," Callie said finally, thinking of the way her mother had cupped the blooms, the risk growers took with the delicate, short-living plants. Wasn't that what life was about, though? Taking a risk, while living loud and vibrant, like the lilies did? "That's what I want to plant. They're not so easy to grow out here, and they'll take a lot of care, but—"

"You like a challenge," Belle finished. She smiled, then gathered Callie into a hug, one that was as comforting as peach pie and ice cream. "I'm glad you're staying, darlin'. The place just wouldn't be the same without your sunshine."

Callie held onto Belle long enough to savor the sweet moment. Then she heard the roar of a familiar motorcycle engine. Callie broke away from Belle, dread multiplying in her stomach.

She drew back the curtain, peeked out the window. When the motorcycle's rider swung off the bike and Callie saw who it was, she realized that sometimes you couldn't run from your problems—

Because they showed up on the front porch instead.

The motorcycle sitting outside the Wedding Belles shop should have been Jared's first clue that disaster loomed. But he walked right past it, a spring in his step, the song Callie had sung the night before still playing in his veins, his mind entirely focused on finding Callie.

Once he'd talked to Pope, he'd turned off the analytic side of his mind, so Jared didn't process the Harley. He was too wrapped up in his internal speech, how he intended to tell Callie he was done researching their relationship. No more testing the hypothesis of love, stacking the statistics and weighing the facts.

From here on out, he was leaping off the bridge of taking chances. Love was a risk—

One Jared was willing to take. Consequences be damned.

He opened the door to the Belles, a ready smile on his face, a smile that died, falling from his face the second his gaze connected with—

Tony's.

"Well, hey, what a blast from the past." Tony rose from the settee, sticking out in the elegant room like tumbleweed in a rose garden and crossed to Jared, clapping him on the back. As if they were still best friends, as if not a day had passed since they'd last seen each other. "How you been, pal?"

"Fine. You?" Jared couldn't manage any more. Couldn't think of what would possibly be polite, socially correct to say, in this situation.

Had Callie invited Tony here? Had he simply shown up out of the blue?

Whatever the case, Tony hadn't aged a bit. He still had that daredevil glint in his eye, the rugged looks of a man who lived by the seat of his pants. Leather jacket, low-slung jeans, a faint growth of beard, a trim, neat body. The scent of cigarettes hung in the air around him. "I'm the same as always. Trying to get into as much trouble as possible without getting caught." Tony laughed. "Came by to see my girl, see what she's up to."

His girl. They were divorced, and yet Tony still laid claim to Callie. Because there was still something between them?

As if drummed up by his thoughts, Callie rounded the corner and came into the room. She stopped cold when she noticed Jared and Tony, together. "Oh, Jared. I, ah, didn't expect you today."

"Apparently. I thought I'd surprise you. I guess I did." He looked from her to Tony, seeing the past replay itself all over again. What did he need to get the hint that she wanted the opposite kind of man to what he was? A billboard? A tractor trailer truck full of signs? "I can see you're busy. I'll talk to you later." Or never.

Jared turned to go. There wasn't any point in staying. He knew that from past experience. Whenever Tony walked into the room, Jared became invisible. Mr. Cool versus Mr. Straight-and-Narrow. Leather won out every time.

Jared made it as far as the door; even let it shut behind him.

Then he wondered what the hell he was doing. Inside that room was a woman he cared about. A woman who was talking to the very man who had broken her heart. A man who had jerk written all over him. If Jared let her stay there and talk to him—maybe even fall under Tony's spell again—what kind of man would he be?

Even if she didn't care about Jared, *he* cared about her, and he owed her a warning, protection from a man like Tony. That much at least.

Who was he kidding? He'd walked out of that

wedding last night, thinking he was doing the best thing for her—

And cursing himself every step of the way.

He wasn't going to do it again.

Jared spun on his heel, flung open the door and nearly collided with Callie. "Don't do it," he said.

"Don't do what?"

"Don't get back together with him. He's no good for you. Hell, he's never been good for you and you know it."

She put her hands on her hips. "Are you telling me what to do?"

"Yeah, I am. And I'm telling you that you should start thinking with your brain and look for a man who actually treasures you and won't crush your heart like a used soda can."

She glared at him. "Who do you think you are?"

"Someone who cares about you. A good friend."

"That's all?" Her eyes sparked like firecrackers. "A good friend?"

"Isn't that what I've always been to you?" He let out a frustrated gust. "A good friend?"

"Well thank you for the advice, Jared, but I am fully capable of making my own decisions. I don't need you to rush in like Sir Galahad. And I don't need another *friend*."

What was it with this woman? She made him completely insane. He'd come over here, intending to tell her how he felt, to ask her to take that risk with him, and now here she was, reinforcing the whole argument they'd had nine years ago. "You're not seriously considering getting back together with Tony, are you?"

"Last I checked, I didn't have to run my love life decisions by you." She pursed her lips, her gaze sweeping over him. "Unless that's part of your research project, too."

"No, I'm done researching love. I've drawn all the conclusions I need. Some that I'm not too happy about, but that's how it goes with research. Sometimes, the results aren't what you'd expect."

"No, they're not. And you know, while we're on that subject, you didn't quite turn out the way I'd expected, either."

He jerked back, surprised. "What do you mean?"

"What happened to the Jared Townsend who had dreams and plans? Because he seems to have disappeared as far as I can tell. I remember that conversation we had the morning after we made love. Do you?"

"Of course I do." He remembered everything about that night—and the next morning.

"You were filled with ideas for your future," she went on. "It was a lot more than the talk about wanting to get married, buy a house, with a garden and a dog. But then you just assumed I wouldn't be interested in that kind of life, Jared."

His mouth opened, closed.

She went on, barreling forward, not waiting for a response. "Maybe I would have said no. Maybe I would have run for the hills. The point is you never gave me a chance to make that choice. But you went on and on, saying you wanted to travel, to jump out of airplanes. To try new things. In the end, you didn't do any of that. You criticize me for running, but at least I'm moving. All you've done is stagnate."

He turned away from her. "I had my reasons."

"Like what, Jared?" She took a step closer to him, coming around to face him again, confronting him. "Why didn't you ever tell me what they were? Why keep it all locked inside?"

"What good was that going to do?" he asked. "Are you going to suddenly change how you feel about me because you found out that I grew up with an alcoholic father? A mother who spent more time with her boyfriends than with me? That my father died when I was seventeen and all of a sudden I was the man of the house? That I became super responsible because I had no choice?"

Her jaw dropped. "I never knew. I'm sorry."

"That's why I needed you as a friend," he said softly, realizing now how much he valued her friendship back then, her quiet presence. Maybe he should have opened up all those years ago. "That's why you were so important to me."

"But why not say anything? That's what friends are for."

"I didn't want your pity, Callie. And besides, I didn't need to tell you," he said, his voice a raw thing that scraped past his throat. "Just having you there in school, and on campus, was enough. You were this…wild thing that gave me hope that someday, down the road, maybe I could do those things, too. To take chances, answer to nobody's clock but my own."

"But you never did."

He sighed. "My mother got sick. Cancer. I needed a dependable job with benefits and a regular paycheck. I ended up becoming your neighborhood bedroom game researcher. Nothing to brag about, but it paid the bills. And after she died last year, it was easier to stay than to jump off the bridge and take a risk." He tipped her chin, studied the green eyes he had known so long, the eyes that both drove him wild and made him want a life he had thus far denied himself. "Until I saw you again."

A smile curved up her face, one filled with understanding, compassion. "Kind of like handing someone a microphone and then leaving them?"

"I was giving you what you wanted, Callie." He inhaled the scent of her perfume, its intoxicating scent driving him crazy at the same time it made him want her in ways he couldn't even count. Damn. How could he walk away? "A way out."

"An escape, you mean."

"The last thing you ever wanted was someone tying you down, isn't that right?" He waved toward the shop. "Isn't that what Tony's all about? No real ties, no real commitment? That's why you chose him over me. Then and now."

"So you were just going to let me go? Be the big sacrificer again?" She let out a gust. "Is that what you wanted? This time, too?"

"Hell, no, Callie."

"Then stop being so damned nice and noble, Jared." She stepped back, away from him, threw up her hands.

Everything within him rose to a boil, not in anger, but in a heated rush of want. He could barely hold back from the desire to swoop down and kiss her, hold her to him and not let her go until the heat had subsided.

She didn't want him to be nice, to be noble. And yet, those were the very qualities in a man that she deserved. The very kind of man that the Callie he knew and loved should have.

The man she'd once married—the man she'd

chosen over him time and time again—was mere feet away. Jared knew that given half the chance, Callie would choose him again. She'd already made that clear by reminding him of their friendship.

She didn't need another friend, she'd said.

Another friend.

No, she didn't need another friend, damn it, and neither did he. He was done being Callie's friend, and if he destroyed that friendship with what he was about to do, then so be it.

"What *are* you really here for, Jared?" she asked.

"This," he said, and he stepped forward, crushed her to him and kissed her more thoroughly and deeply than he ever had before in one long, hot second that took his breath away. His tongue slipped into her mouth, invited hers to dance, and she did, her arms going around his body, her mouth opening wider, a slight moan escaping her throat, and she seemed to go liquid in his arms. Their kiss deepened, and he cupped her jaw, tracing the delicate outline of her face with his thumbs, memorizing every inch of her. When the fire in his gut reached a roar, Jared stepped back, the world spinning for a second, then let her go.

Callie blinked, then drew in a shudder of a breath. "What was that for?"

"An experiment," Jared said. "To test my hypothesis about friendship."

"Friends don't kiss each other like that."

"I don't want to be your friend. Not for one more day, damn it. In fact, we are officially done being friends."

Her mouth opened in surprise, but he cut off her words by trailing a finger along her jaw. Every touch of her silken skin made him want her even more now than he had five seconds ago. "I've wanted you from the first moment I met you, Callie. But I lied to you about what I wanted you for." He cupped her chin, his gaze meeting hers. "I want it all, Callie. I still want the house, the picket fence, the kids, the Labrador. But I want *you* in that house with me. Because I love you. I have always loved you. I loved you when you were making those aprons in home ec. When you were quoting Macbeth, when you were singing Madonna songs, when you were arranging tulips. I love you, Callie, and I want more than friendship."

"Jared—" Her eyes widened, and he knew he'd pushed it too far, too fast.

Damn, he'd done it again. He should know better. Should have learned from his mistakes. Nine years ago, he'd said nearly the same words and Callie had bolted from his bed like she'd been on fire. Running straight into Tony's arms.

But if he stopped now, where would that leave him? Going home to an empty apartment, wondering what if. With a bunch of regrets, and another nine years ahead of him without her.

Nope. Not this time. Jared was getting on the Tilt-A-Whirl and not getting off until he had the answer he wanted. And if he didn't get it, at least he'd know he'd jumped.

He reached into his back pocket and pulled out the plane tickets he'd bought a few days earlier. "Here are two plane tickets to Mexico. I paid for one of those adventure weekends in Cozumel. Skyline riding, ATV rentals, snorkeling, jet skiing, you name the adventure, it's on the ticket."

She stared at them, then at him. "What is this about?"

"I want you to go with me, Callie. Not to run away forever, but for a vacation. The way normal people do it. Then, we come back here, go to work. Well, I start looking for work," he chuckled, "and then we start planning our wedding."

He'd already given her the big scare. Might as well go all in.

She gasped. "Are you…asking me to marry you?"

"Yes, I am." He reached up, loosened his necktie, tugged it off and threw the slip of silk to the ground. "I am tired of being dependable, predictable, nice Jared. I want to be the man who sweeps you off your feet and surprises the hell out of you." Then he dropped to one knee, fished the ring he'd bought the same day as the plane tickets out of his pocket and flipped open the velvet box. The marquis-cut stone and the two smaller stones on either side winked back the sun's reflection. "Callie, I'm asking you to take the biggest risk of all. Will you marry me?"

"You making a pass at my girl?"

Tony's voice was all joke, but the underlying meaning was not. Callie knew that tone.

She spun around, angry at the intrusion, the implication. "Tony, I'm not your girl anymore."

He trundled down the stairs, shot Jared a glare, then slipped in beside Callie. "Sure you are," he said, his arm curling around her waist with a possessiveness that she hated. "You always have been."

Jared rose, the ring box closing with a snap. "Tony, Callie and I were talking."

"Yeah, well I was here first. And she is my wife."

"*Ex,*" Callie stressed. She stepped out of Tony's embrace. "I'm not your girl and I never was. You cheated on me, Tony. Remember? Not just once, but dozens of times. You had all the loyalty of a stray dog."

"Callie, we might have had our disagreements—"

"Disagreements?" Her voice rose. "You left me the minute we moved to Boston to go live with your girlfriend. A girlfriend who *followed* you to Boston, if you remember correctly. Because you asked her to. That was a nice little surprise for me." She shook her head, the familiar disgust returning. How could she have been so stupid, so blinded to a man who had said all the right things, but done all the wrong ones behind her back? "I don't know why I stayed married to you as long as I did. Why I even fell for you in the first place."

But she did know. She'd kept hoping that the words he'd spoken would be true. That the lies would somehow turn around. That someday, Tony would turn into the hero she'd made him out to be in her mind. The bigger than life guy on the motorcycle, Mr. Wild, who would take her away from the upside-down life she'd hated so much. If he had become that man, she wouldn't have had to face the fact that she had made one colossal mistake with her life.

Tony scowled. "Jared, give us some privacy, will ya? Me and Callie, we have things to work out." Tony arched a brow. "If you know what I mean."

Jared looked at Callie, standing his ground. "Do you want me to leave?"

The fact that Jared was willing to stay was enough. But she was a big girl, and she had to settle this with Tony once and for all at some point. It would be easier to do it without a third party around.

And, she needed time. Time to consider the question Jared had asked her. A question she didn't know how to answer. "Can I call you later?"

Jared looked from Tony to Callie, then back again. "Sure. I'll be at O'Malley's."

Jared walked away, and Callie knew she'd done something wrong. Hurt him again. Somehow it seemed no matter how she handled this situation, she did it wrong.

Damn.

But what was she supposed to do? She hadn't been expecting Jared to whip out two plane tickets and a marriage proposal. Her mind was a whirlwind. What did she want? Should she even marry again? Considering she was standing beside her biggest marital mistake?

Tony shrugged, nonplussed by Jared's departure. He crossed to the building's stoop, sat down on the step, laid back, arms outstretched, legs crossed. "So, babe, I'm back in town," he said, talking as if nothing had happened, that they were just picking up after a day apart, "and I'm thinking of going down to Mexico. There's this guy down there, runs a fishing operation. Has a hut on the beach, easy living, easy money. Drinking margaritas all day. And I need a partner." Tony gave her the familiar grin that had talked her into everything from spending a year living out of an RV to six months of backpacking through the Sierras. "What do you say? One more adventure for you and me?"

She considered Tony, and wondered what she had ever seen in him. Once, he had been handsome to her. But now all she saw was a cocky grin and brown eyes with lonely depths. "That life isn't for me anymore."

"What, you like this nine to five grind?" He let out a snort. "Or with these wedding people, I bet it's more like every weekend, too. They're demanding as hell, from what I see on TV. That's gotta suck."

"Actually it's fun. I really enjoy it."

"Right. You told me once that staying in the same place for more than a few months makes you crazy. You're made for the open road, baby. You're not a stick-to-anything kind of girl."

She shook her head. "I am now, Tony. I like it here. I have a career. A life."

Tony's brown eyes studied her for a long time, then his gaze narrowed. "Oh, I get it. The professor there, he's the kind of guy you want? You throwing me over for the old friend, is that it?"

"I might."

Tony scoffed. "Come on. Five minutes of 'How do you want your eggs?' and 'Pass me the Sunday crossword' and you'll be out of there. I know you, Callie, and I know Jared. That kind of thing—his kind of dull—drives you crazy." He mocked a yawn and shook his head.

"No, it doesn't. Maybe in the old days, but not now." She thought of the Jared she'd gotten to know lately and knew there hadn't been anything dull at all about the feelings he'd awakened in her.

In fact, he had been a grown-up kind of relationship, one where she'd been able to talk, to share her dreams, her work. She'd never done that with Tony, never had him listen to anything that interested her. Instead it had been her following him on one crazy idea after another, thinking that she was happy.

When all she'd been doing was searching for happiness—and never finding it.

Tony popped forward on the step, his eyes bright. "Tell me you haven't gotten the itch lately. Tell me you haven't thought a hundred times about ditching this place and running off to Tahiti or Alaska or San Tropez."

The places rattled off his tongue with the tempting whisper of a man who had been to those exotic locales, a man who knew which buttons to push in Callie's psyche.

For a split second, the wanderlust roared inside her, the images of the places popping up like slides on a screen. Tony may have been a horrible husband, but he knew her well. Knew the constant craving for something new that ran through her veins, like a third blood cell. "They need me here, Tony. I can't just up—"

Tony rose, crossed to her, taking her hand. "Screw those people. Come with me. I need you, too."

Come with me. I need you. A hundred times before, those were the words that had convinced Callie to take one trip after another, brought her from city to city, tagging along with Tony, talked her into dropping out of college, leaving her hometown, never buying a house—never signing anything more permanent than a month-to-month lease. She'd never owned a dog, a cat or even a potted plant. Not until she'd started working for Belle.

But now she wanted to stay, wanted to plant that garden, those lilies. Running had never gotten her anywhere but away from a home.

"Come with me," Tony whispered again, his mouth nuzzling along her neck.

Callie jumped away. "No. I don't want that life.

I stopped loving you a long time ago and I stopped loving living like that."

Shock widened his eyes. "You're serious, babe?"

"Yes. All these years, I kept holding the idea of leaving Boston like a trap door I could slip through when things got too scary. And here you come along, offering me that door and guess what? I don't want it. I like what I have here. I can go to Tahiti and San Tropez. On *vacation*."

He snorted. "Are you kidding me? You're seriously going to stay here?"

She nodded, grinning like a fool. "Yep. But first, I have to buy a leash."

"A leash?" Tony stared at her. "What the hell do you need a—"

But Callie was already gone.

CHAPTER THIRTEEN

"You missing something?"

Jared looked up from the beer that had been sitting in front of him for a good ten minutes and had yet to be touched, to find the bartender at O'Malley's grinning at him. "Missing something?"

O'Malley leaned over the pint glasses before him, gesturing at Jared. "You're the clipboard guy Callie was with, right? Women find statistics sexy and all that?"

"Oh, yeah." Jared toyed with the rim of the mug and shook his head. "But I'm done with that job."

"What was that all about anyway?" O'Malley stood up, then swiped at the counter, cleaning up the circular imprints left by earlier drinks. Even though it was midafternoon, the bar was quite busy, a low hum of conversation carrying across the room from the several filled tables. An Eagles song played on the jukebox, and a couple slow danced to the tune in the middle of the floor.

"Love. I was researching love."

"You learn anything?"

Jared snorted. "Given the results? I don't think so."

O'Malley laughed. "I don't know about that. I think you did pretty good, actually, at least when it comes to relationships with people." He jerked his head to the right. "Have you met my new short-order cook?"

Jared followed O'Malley's direction, then sat back in surprise. "Sam?"

The older man crossed the room, a smile taking over his face, lighting up his clear, bright eyes. No longer drunk, but sober and neat as a pin, wearing an apron, jeans and a denim shirt. "Hey, Jared! I've been hoping you'd come back in. Been wanting to thank you."

"You're working here?" Jared couldn't have been more surprised if Sam had knocked him over with a keg.

Sam nodded. "I took your advice. Cleaned myself up, got a job. Thought I'd start here, since this is kind of where I found my miracle, and a Help Wanted sign." He chuckled.

"Best thing I ever did, hiring him," the bartender said. "Who knew adding spaghetti carbonara and grilled chicken sandwiches to my afternoon menu could boost business so much?"

"I did," Sam said, shooting O'Malley a grin, before turning back to Jared. "We jazzed up the menu, tweaking a few things here and there. Nothing motivates a man like feeling useful again. I missed my restaurant and it was sure nice to get behind a stove again."

"I'm glad for you," Jared said.

Sam studied him, turning the dish towel in his hands over and over. "Why did you help me that night? I was just a sloppy drunk sitting at the end of the bar."

"My dad," Jared began. He paused for a second, then continued. "My dad had a drinking problem. Maybe if someone had talked to him, he might have…"

"Wised up before it was too late?"

Jared nodded.

Sam slipped onto the stool beside Jared and laid a hand on Jared's shoulder. The older man's touch offered a balm that seemed to reach across the years, as if soothing a wound left over from Jared's childhood, and Jared knew why he had helped Sam. Why it made him feel so good to see Sam sober, working. "I'm sorry for you, son," Sam said. "But if it's any help, because of you, I'm mending the fences with my kids and my grand-kids."

"It does," Jared said. "More than you know." It

might be too late with his parents, but at least he could see one happy ending here. "Thank you, Sam."

"Thank me? For what?" Sam laughed. "I didn't do anything."

"Oh, you did," Jared said. "You did."

The bartender cleared his throat. "Guess you didn't need the clipboard after all. What is it with you professor types? Is it the glasses?"

Jared looked up at O'Malley, then saw that he was pointing toward the door.

"I heard there's a man in here who knows what makes a woman's heart sing."

Jared turned at the sound of Callie's voice, his pulse going from zero to sixty in the time it took him to make the half circle spin. Part of him hadn't expected to see her, and the other part—

Well, it had been hoping like a five-year-old at Christmas.

"I was in the neighborhood," she said, a smile playing across her lips. She crossed to him, looking beautiful, as always. "Want to get some sun, Dracula?"

He grinned, slipped off the stool. "Sure."

Sam and O'Malley exchanged smiles. Jared went to pay his tab, but O'Malley waved it off. "You're welcome here anytime," O'Malley said.

A moment later, Jared and Callie were outside,

enjoying a warm April day. They strolled down the sidewalk, faces upturned to the sun. He took her hand in his, the feel of her palm as natural as anything he'd ever known. "Where's Tony?"

She shrugged. "Halfway to Mexico, I guess."

"And you're not?"

"I have better things to stay for."

Hope soared in his chest, but he tamped it down. Jared had always been a realist, and he wasn't about to change today. Not yet. "Are you going to keep working for Belle?"

Callie paused on the sidewalk, swinging into Jared's arms. She shook her head, teasing him. "Are you going to keep talking around the subject?"

"What subject would that be?"

"If I remember right, you asked me a question. A very important, life altering question. And I didn't answer it."

He grinned, felt the smile reach all the way through his veins, down into his gut. "No, you didn't."

"First, I have something to tell you." She took a step closer, grasping his other hand with hers. Her green eyes met his, clear and direct. "All my life, I've been afraid of really committing to anyone, so I did the next worst thing. I married a man who was just like my father. A man who wouldn't stay committed. Of course I didn't realize it at the time, but now that this particular scarecrow got some brains, I see my mistakes a little better."

"In science, we don't call them mistakes. They're part of the learning curve."

She laughed. "Well, it took me a long time to go around that curve. I was so afraid of what might happen if I screwed up again, I just…didn't get involved. Didn't fall in love." She tiptoed a finger up his lips. "Until now."

He swallowed, dared to allow hope to rise even higher. "Until now?"

She nodded. "I love you, Jared. I think I always have, I've just been too afraid to admit it. I love the way you look in a tie. I love that you fiddle with your glasses when you're nervous. I love the way you try to sing. And I especially love the way you kiss me."

He grinned, then lowered his mouth within kissing distance. "You do, do you?"

"Uh-huh."

So he kissed her, just to make sure that she loved that particular kiss, too. Given the way she reacted, he'd say he'd struck gold again. He took his time savoring her lips, tasting the sweetness of her, enjoying every moment of her touch. He'd never imagined there could be anything as wonderful as kissing a woman he had known for so many years.

Maybe that was what gave it the sweetness. Knowing her so well, being able to predict the movements of her lips, her head, her hands. He knew the curve of her jaw, the touch of skin, the scent of her perfume, as well as he knew his own hands.

"Oh, Callie," he murmured, then pulled back, thinking there was nothing more beautiful than the emerald depths of Callie's eyes. "So, now that you've found your Mr. Right, what are you going to do with him?"

She grinned. "Oh, I'm going to marry him. But he'll have to wait a little bit. Someone has to get housebroken first so we can go on our honeymoon and not worry about the carpet."

Jared arched a brow. "Housebroken?"

Callie laughed, then stepped out of Jared's arms and over to her car. She thumbed the remote, unlocking it. Jared noticed the windows were slightly open and a…whimpering was coming from inside the vehicle. "I decided you might want a little proof that I'm here to stay." She opened up the passenger's side door of the Toyota, and out bounded a golden retriever puppy, whose massive paws scrambled across the sidewalk, then up Jared's pants, leaving a dusting of fur. Callie grabbed the leash attached to the dog's collar and got the puppy to halfway sit.

"We can't settle down unless we have a house, a garden and a dog."

That had been exactly what they'd talked about all those years ago in her bed, when he'd told her his dream of the perfect life. A house. A garden. A dog. And a wife.

This wife, in particular.

Happiness erupted in Jared's chest, and he took her hand, then pressed a kiss to Callie's lips. "Training a puppy might put a serious crimp in our travel plans."

"I know," Callie said, laughing and smiling. "And I don't care. I have everything I need right here." Then she curved into Jared's arms, finding home right where she stood.

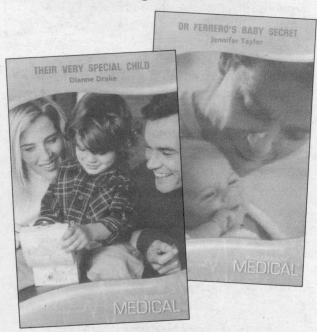

Celebrate 100 years of pure reading pleasure with Mills & Boon®

To mark our centenary, each month we're publishing a special 100th Birthday Edition. These celebratory editions are packed with extra features and include a FREE bonus story.

Plus, starting in February you'll have the chance to enter a fabulous monthly prize draw. See 100th Birthday Edition books for details.

Now that's worth celebrating!

15th February 2008

Raintree: Inferno by Linda Howard
Includes FREE bonus story Loving Evangeline
A double dose of Linda Howard's heady mix of passion and adventure

4th April 2008

The Guardian's Forbidden Mistress by Miranda Lee
Includes FREE bonus story The Magnate's Mistress
Two glamorous and sensual reads from favourite author Miranda Lee!

2nd May 2008

The Last Rake in London by Nicola Cornick
Includes FREE bonus story The Notorious Lord
Lose yourself in two tales of high society and rakish seduction!

Look for Mills & Boon 100th Birthday Editions at your favourite bookseller or visit
www.millsandboon.co.uk

0108/CENTENARY_2-IN-1

4 FREE

BOOKS AND A SURPRISE GIFT!

We would like to take this opportunity to thank you for reading this Mills & Boon® book by offering you the chance to take FOUR more specially selected titles from the Romance series absolutely FREE! We're also making this offer to introduce you to the benefits of the Mills & Boon® Reader Service™—

- ★ **FREE home delivery**
- ★ **FREE gifts and competitions**
- ★ **FREE monthly Newsletter**
- ★ **Exclusive Reader Service offers**
- ★ **Books available before they're in the shops**

Accepting these FREE books and gift places you under no obligation to buy, you may cancel at any time, even after receiving your free shipment. Simply complete your details below and return the entire page to the address below. You don't even need a stamp!

YES! Please send me 4 free Romance books and a surprise gift. I understand that unless you hear from me, I will receive 6 superb new titles every month for just £2.99 each, postage and packing free. I am under no obligation to purchase any books and may cancel my subscription at any time. The free books and gift will be mine to keep in any case.

N8ZED

Ms/Mrs/Miss/Mr ....Initials ....

BLOCK CAPITALS PLEASE

Surname ....

Address ....

....

..................................Postcode.......................................

Send this whole page to:
UK: FREEPOST CN81, Croydon, CR9 3WZ